Infradead:
Tales of Human Extinction

Features
44   Movie Review: Leave the World Behind by Lee Clark Zumpe

Short Stories
6   The Dustbin by Tyree Campbell
25   The Ten Plagues by Josh Schlossberg
54   They Came In Peace by John Darling
66   Die With Dignity by Tyree Campbell

Flash Fiction
22   Looking Down to Look Up by Joseph Farley
52   Loyal Employee by Rob McMonigal

Poems
19   Held Over Indefinitely by G. O. Clark
50   Mother by Christopher Hivner

THE STAFF OF HIRAETH PUBLISHING

EDITOR: Tyree Campbell
WEBMASTER: H David Blalock
STAFF EDITORS:
Terrie Leigh Relf
Teri Santitoro
Marcie Lynn Tentchoff
H David Blalock
Christina Sng
Bad Bob Bellam

Copyrights owned by the respective authors and artists
Cover art "Empty House" and cover design by Marcia A. Borell

All rights reserved. No part of this book may be reproduced or transmitted in any form or by any means, electronic or mechanical, including photocopying or recording or by any information storage and retrieval systems, without expressed written consent of the author and/or artists.

Infradead is a work of fiction. Names, characters, places, and incidents are products of the author's imagination. Any resemblance to actual events or persons, living or dead, is entirely coincidental.

First Printing, August 2024

Hiraeth Publishing
P.O. Box 1248
Tularosa, NM 88352
e-mail: hiraethsubs@yahoo.com

Visit www.hiraethsff.com for online science fiction, fantasy, horror, scifaiku, and more. Stop by our online bookstore for novels, magazines, anthologies, and collections. **Support the small, independent press...and your First Amendment rights.**

A Little Help, Please

In the world of the small indie press we fight a never-ending battle for attention to our work, as writers and in publishing. Here's an example: big publishers [you know who they are] have gobs of $$$ that they can devote to advertising and marketing. Here at Hiraeth Publishing, our advertising budget consists of the deposits for whatever soda bottles and aluminum cans we can find alongside the highways. Anti-littering laws make our task even more difficult . . . ☺

That's where YOU come in. YOU are our best promoter. YOU are the one who can tell others about us. Just send 'em to our website, tell them about our store. That's all. Just that.

Of course, we don't mind if you talk us up. We're pretty good, you know. We have some award-winning and award-nominated writers and artists, plus other voices well-deserving to be heard [not everyone wins awards, right?] but our publications are read-worthy nevertheless.

That number once again is:
www.hiraethsffh.com

Friend us on Facebook at Hiraeth Publishing
Follow us on Twitter at @HiraethPublish1

Sarrow

By Tyree Campbell

The oceans have evaporated as the Earth warmed. It is a time of desolation as the remnants of humanity live in small settlements scattered on what once was the ocean floor. Men are paramount, women are breeders. People do what they can to get by.

One breeder dares to say "No!" to all this: Sarrow. Refusing to breed, and more skilled and resourceful than most men, she sets off to seek her identity and her destiny. Along the way she encounters Karthan, a kindred spirit. Like her, he searches for himself. They are equals.

But the elements conspire against them: earthquakes, salt storms, volcanoes, flash floods. And there are raiding parties who seek to capture and sell slaves. Where are Sarrow and Karthan to go?

Up, says Sarrow. I believe in you, says Karthan. Thus the perilous journey back to the land begins.

https://www.hiraethsffh.com/product-page/sarrow-by-tyree-campbell

The Dustbin
Tyree Campbell

As Pierce reached the crest of the hill he caught a flash of pale flesh, a spark of hair the color of fresh copper, moving fast through the forest several hundred yards away. The glimpse was enough to give him the impression of the runner as a woman, supple and slender. He heard shouts, a rifle firing. Soldiers had flushed their quarry and were running her to ground.

Ahead was a Y intersection, the two dirt roads leading along the north and south slopes of the valley. She was running toward the south. The soldiers, then, had come from the north. Pierce knew that road, and surmised that they had stopped along the shoulder on the rise to the bridge that crossed the river. Since the end of the Wisconsin glaciation the river had cut through limestone on its way down the valley to the Missouri River. Likely the woman lived in one of the caves, fishing the river, perhaps husbanding a dispersed kitchen garden. Now that part of her life was over. Without his intervention, probably all of it was.

It was not his concern. People died every day by murder or misadventure. Weariness in his very bones made it easy for him to dismiss her plight. His five-year quest for revenge completed now, he longed for nothing but a peaceful place to lie down and pass on. He was done with it. *Done with it.*

Still he looked. She continued to flee.

Five years in paramilitary service had familiarized Pierce with all the good words, and he knew how to cluster them together with hyphens for best effect. Several of them seethed from his mouth as he slammed the gearshift into second, flattened the accelerator, and gunned the jeep down the hill and onto the south road. In decades past the county would have dispatched road crews to spread fresh gravel, trim back the trees, and mow the grass and wildflowers that grew along the roadside. Nowadays the road passed through a tunnel of vegetation, dark as dusk, before it emerged into the valley on the other side of the forest. The jeep's shocks were more than a match for the uneven surface, and Pierce pushed the vehicle past forty, gripping the steering wheel with hands at ten minutes to two, as the manual recommended and as few people heeded, fighting with the wheel as potholes and ruts tried to alter his course. If the woman kept to her pace and direction, and if she weren't caught or shot, she would reach the south road in another minute, perhaps less. Over the noise of travel he heard another shot. A single shot, not automatic fire: they weren't trying to kill her, merely to wound her or to bring her to a halt. If possible, she was to be taken alive—although perhaps to some of the soldiers her condition upon capture would not have dampened their interest.

At the bottom of the hill Pierce rounded a gentle curve where the elevated roadbed took him a dozen feet above the forest floor. A sharp turn of the wheel and a firm boot on the brakes sent the jeep onto the graveled shoulder on the oncoming side of the road, the north side, where he reckoned the woman would emerge. With the gearshift in neutral and the idle low, he cocked an ear, listening. The forest here was almost black some five yards into it, so thick was the vegetation, but Pierce thought he heard muffled thrashing, a body thrusting past leaves and branches. A shout, and another. Probably by this time her pursuers were closing on her. He squinted, seeking nuances of movement through the leaves, swatches of pale flesh through the trees. She had to be in there somewhere.

Suddenly she was there, as if she had materialized at the bottom of the slope. She rushed up the incline toward him, just as two of her pursuers emerged from the forest with rifles at port. Already Pierce had unslung the pump-action crossbow and nocked a bolt. Her climb blocked his view of the soldiers, and his aim.

He barely had time to register that the oncoming young woman was worth looking at. The flash of her seared his mind. Tallish, slender, breasts the size of oranges and as firm, full pubic ruff almost as coppery as her hair, pale skin splashed all over with large, pale freckles, eyes dark in the shadows, though they might be green, thin lips slightly parted to draw the breaths necessary to maintain her flight, hair and body wet as if she had been bathing when flushed out by the soldiers, eyes wide and then narrow as she found him and took him in.

"*Down,*" he yelled, and immediately she spilled forward onto the lush wildflowers. The implicit trust astonished Pierce, but he had no time to evaluate it. He aimed, fired, drew the cocking slide to nock another bolt, aimed, and fired. *Thung snick snick thung.* Neither soldier had time to bring his rifle to bear before the envenomed shaft struck him in the face, where the skin was bare. Both pitched forward directly they were struck.

"*Climb in,*" Pierce yelled, still aiming at the forest.

The young woman rose and scrambled up the remaining slope and into the back of the jeep, clambering over the passenger seat to sit down beside him. Already Pierce had the vehicle in motion, his eyes both on the road and in the rearview mirror. The woman reached behind the seat and seized the M16 there, and the two thirty-round banana clips duct-taped together. While Pierce sent the jeep hurtling through the tunnel of overhanging branches, she cleared the weapon, inserted the clip, and chambered a round—left-handed, Pierce noted—and took up a watch aft, protecting against pursuit. She was mumbling to herself, barely audible, but enough to tell Pierce that she knew some good words, too.

The road gave onto the valley without warning. In one moment, the forest concealed them; in the next, they were exposed. Almost as if the soldiers had been waiting for their emergence, a mortar round erupted a hundred yards short of the road several seconds later. Pierce flinched, but kept driving. The woman twisted in the seat and brought the rifle to bear on the bridge almost a thousand yards away. Pierce glanced at the bridge. A covered deuce-and-a-half truck was parked just short of it, and several soldiers were pointing their rifles toward the road. Pierce heard the tell-tale *crumpf* of a mortar being fired, and this time the round landed closer by half. A few shards of metal struck the jeep. One sliced across the point of the woman's left shoulder, and a line of blood welled. The wound was not deep, and she made no sound of complaint, or gave any sign that she was in pain.

Clearly she wanted to return fire with the rifle, but that meant firing directly above Pierce's head.

Another glance told Pierce that the soldiers were reboarding the truck. Evidently they meant to challenge the woman's escape by taking the valley's north road until they gained a more favorable position. Pierce pulled the jeep to the far side of the road and stopped. While the woman looked a question at him, he unlocked the magazine of bolts from the crossbow and inserted another magazine, cocking a fresh bolt into place, this one a much darker brown than its predecessors. As he climbed out of the jeep, the woman came around the front of it.

Pierce took aim at the far abutment of the bridge just as the woman began firing. The unanticipated reports of the rifle distracted him, and when he turned his head to look at her, the view of her took his breath away.

She was standing frontally toward him with her feet shoulder-width apart, wet copper hair plastered to her shoulders and back, the butt of the M16 socketed into the corner of her left shoulder, right arm bent, rifle barrel fitted into the V of her right thumb and fingers, left cheek against the stock, sighting at the bridge and the soldiers on it. Carefully she squeezed off round after round, her breasts below the rifle trembling slightly with each recoil.

Pierce lowered the crossbow. The sight of the woman—her nakedness, her open posture, her combativeness—had aroused him to the point where he wanted nothing more than to mount her, right then and there. A hard ache in his chest reminded him that he needed to breathe, and he drew a sharp inhalation and returned his attention to the abutment. A soldier fell from the bridge into the river twenty yards below. Seconds later, after Pierce had sent two bolts flying toward the abutment, they heard his scream. The woman emptied one magazine, removed and reversed it, reloaded, and continued firing, this time at the covered back of the truck, which was now beginning to move across the bridge. Pierce sent three more bolts into the abutment, then thumbed a button on the side of the crossbow. Immediately a great gout of orange erupted at the joint of the bridge and the abutment, and that end of the bridge collapsed. The truck and several soldiers on foot tumbled into the river.

A third mortar round fell, this one far short of the road. Pierce boarded the jeep, and the woman reluctantly joined him. With one hand on the wheel, Pierce replaced the new magazine of crossbow bolts with the old one, folded the wings of the crossbow, and slid the weapon into a sleeve alongside the back of the seat. The woman set the safety on the rifle and returned it to the back seat.

Aware that she was watching him intently, Pierce said nothing. In truth he did not know what to say. More than three years had passed since he had had an interaction with a woman that bordered on the sexual, but that was not the cause of his silence. He had the feeling that there was something else that he was supposed to do, that something was not quite right, and he had no idea what it was. He sensed no danger from the woman, yet clearly she was dangerous.

She was sitting with her legs crossed at the ankles and her hands folded demurely in her lap, and she was looking at him in a way that suggested that he was supposed to look at her—this much he saw out of the corner of his eye. But did she expect him to look, or did she want him to look? Either way, why?

They reached a section of the road that was relatively straight for the next few miles. Pierce turned his head to look at her—at her face, at her eyes wide and pale green now, the irises flecked with gold sparks that seemed to dance with mirth—and he was very careful to look directly and only at her face.

"Nice shooting," he said.

The hint of a smile toyed with the corners of her mouth. "I was firing for effect," she told him. Her contralto had just a touch of smoke, as if her throat was dry, and a slight inflection that he could not identify. "I had no real hope of hitting anything at that range."

Pierce returned his eyes to the road ahead. "And yet you hit something."

"I don't mind your looking at me."

Stunned by her candor, Pierce managed to maintain a bland expression. He slowed the jeep to a crawl and turned to look at her: at her face, where for a long moment he saw in her eyes his own reflection; at her left shoulder, where the thin line of blood was already scabbing over; at her breasts, trembling with each pit and pothole the jeep passed over; at the coppery pubic ruff under her folded hands, still moist from her bathing; at her legs, extended deep into the foot well. He did not indulge in a tour of her body so much as demonstrate that her assumption was in error.

"I presume nothing without invitation," he said.

"I'll just have one engraved for you."

A mile of silence followed after he returned the jeep to speed. Without looking at her, he said, "That duffel bag in the back seat has clean clothes you're welcome to. There's an extra pair of boots in the foot well behind your seat that should fit you, albeit loosely."

Deliberately she turned toward him to kneel on the seat, to reach back for the bag, to allow her right breast to nuzzle his shoulder, to make him aware of the proximity of her bare right flank and hip. Pierce was torn between enjoying the contact and wondering why she was doing it to a stranger she had just met. It didn't add up. Most strangers of opposite sexes were far warier.

At last she turned back around and began to dress, neither slowly nor teasingly, but with an economy of movement that nevertheless might have been accompanied by brassy music for disrobing. She had selected an outfit like Pierce's of camouflage tee, jockey briefs, cammie trousers with a black web belt, thick green socks, and the boots he had mentioned. Finished, she spread her hands, inviting his assessment of the result.

Pierce glanced at her but said nothing. Another mile passed.

"You haven't even asked my name," said the woman.

"I don't want to know your name."

The woman's upper incisors caught on her lower lip and nibbled it lightly. Presently she whispered, "That was harsh." As if in defiance of his wishes, she added, "It's Jenny Lee."

The road bent slightly to the north, bringing them closer to the river. They passed the remains of small farms, the skeletons of their barns rotting, their fences in disarray. Stalks of corn grew where the previous year's seed had fallen, and the ears might have been harvested, but there was no one to tend to them. Rats and mice ate the corn, snakes ate the rodents, and raptors ate the snakes. Pierce glanced up: the blue sky was clear of raptors.

Jenny was gazing pensively at the farmland to the south. Weeds had overtaken the dirt roads, which clearly had not been graded since things fell apart. TFA, they called it, thought Pierce, following her gaze. This was the year 24 TFA, or 2110 in old notation. There was no particular day assigned to the collapse; rather, a series of events had occurred, some more disastrous than others, and afterwards the world lay irrevocably changed. Billions were dead. A thousand and more nuclear weapons had been cast here and there, but fewer than half of them actually detonated, as governments had spent more money developing new technologies than they had to maintain the old weaponry. A blessing in disguise, that was, thought Pierce.

There had followed the predictable apocalyptic catastrophe: war, famine, and pestilence riding alongside death. Several countries suffered superbugs, but for the most part biowarfare was superfluous, what with all the typhus and typhoid and even a resurrected smallpox working their evil. Initially famine had been slaked by ransacking the grocery stores, in the U.S. and most other countries. But most folks lived in cities, which were not known for farms and gardens. When the canned supplies were exhausted, people starved. Some managed to find their way to farms, but most of the animals there had perished as well—dairy cows especially, for there was no one to milk them, and their udders burst. All that remained was carrion; vultures were fat.

Still, some areas had more than others. That was when the wars began.

"You're pensive," she said.

As much was evident; Pierce did not respond.

"Okay, I get that you're not happy with me around," she went on. "So what are you going to do with me?"

"Not what you fear, I daresay."

"But you did look."

Pierce rolled his eyes. "*Of course* I looked."

"And?" she prodded.

"Where is this going?"

"Where are *we* going?"

"*We* are going to Aunt Maude's," Pierce replied. "*I* will continue on my way."

"Aunt Maude's."

Pierce sighed. He had no desire to talk with her, and yet he kept responding to her. Months had passed since he had said anything to anyone. He liked it that way. His war was over. It was time to . . . to . . .

"Dammit," he said, and slapped his hand on the steering wheel.

"I did not mean to upset you," she said.

He pursed his lips, blocking a comment. Briefly he considered whether to remain silent. Against his will, he liberated the words. "Maude's is neutral territory, by unspoken agreement," he explained, trying to use as few words as possible. "Folks from The Wastelands stop by, as do the Indian Nations, the GLC, Appalachia, and the CSA. They stop by for peace and quiet on their way from one place to another. Maude takes in strays. She protects them, feeds and clothes them, arranges for their education, and finds work for them to do. There's an old sign on the window by the door. A spotted dog on a yellow background, and the words 'Safe Spot.' No one would violate this place."

"And you're going to leave me there," she said, her voice now as dull as a lead bell.

Her tone clutched at Pierce's heart. She puzzled him; he'd thought she would be grateful.

"Say something!" she snapped.

"You'll be safe there." The words sounded lame in his ears. He glanced at her; quickly she turned her face away, but not before he saw the tear.

He made mental fists. He tried to tell himself he was better off alone; he'd had years of practice at that. But did that signify? *Why* would the woman want *him*? He was almost twice her age, and from a different generation. Or were the generations so different, these days?

With a little snarl of irritation, Pierce pulled the jeep off to the side of the road, where there was enough shoulder for parking. He did not shut the motor off. He leaned back in the seat and twisted a little toward her. She continued to avert her face.

Pierce found a soft tone that he hadn't used in years. "Jenny?"

She turned to look at him. Tears rolled down her cheeks.

Pierce took a deep breath to steady himself. "I'm used to being alone," he told her, as gently as he could. "I'm better off alone."

Jenny blinked. "How would you know, if you haven't been with someone?" she asked him.

He smiled in spite of himself. "A point for you. Jenny—"

"You're not the only one here who has been alone," she broke in, rushing her words as if she were afraid he would cut her off before she got all of them out. "I kept track of the days in my cave by the river. My parents were killed when I was fourteen. We had a secret room underground, where we could go in case of attack or a tornado. You couldn't find it unless you knew exactly where to look for it. That room saved me. I stayed there until the food ran out. Then I found the cave . . ." For a few seconds her face twisted in agony. "Oh, God, my *cave!*" she wailed.

"Jenny—"

She brushed her hand at him. "Eight years there," she went on, her voice choked now. "My drawings, my sketches, my poetry and writing and observations. My work . . . my *life* was in that cave. Gone now, all gone." She fell silent, and he allowed her that, waiting for her. "I-I used to make little whistles from green saplings," she said, as if to herself. "You slide the cylinder of bark free and make a little indentation in the wood, then put the bark back on. Well, there's a little more to it. I never learned to make whistles that had more than one tone, although I'm sure there's a way. So I made eight whistles, one for each note. Sometimes . . . sometimes I would play all day."

"Jenny . . ."

"I had conversations with myself," she said. "Long conversations. The way the river flowed along the banks. The flowers that grew there. A poem by Longfellow; another by Macauley. I had an old copy of Tolstoy's *The Death of Ivan Ilych*, and talked it over with myself after I read it. That's gone, now, too; they destroyed everything I had. Everything I *am*." Thumbing tears away, she peered at him. "Do you have talks with yourself, too?" she asked.

He was forced to admit to himself that he did, more often than he cared to think about. In response, though, he merely nodded.

"Jenny. Why?"

A smile tugged at the corners of her mouth. "Why you?" He nodded again, and she said, "Well . . . you're kind of craggy, and there are more than a few gray hairs in that black mop of yours. You have kind eyes; you're probably not aware of it. But none of that is why. I don't need Apollo. I need to be with someone who makes me feel safe. I need to be with someone who hasn't given up."

"But I *have* given up," said Pierce.

Jenny shook her head. "You rescued me. That's not the act of a man who has given up. And yes, you looked at me. Looked, but made no move whatsoever to touch or to take. That's not the way of a man who has lost his self-respect. No, if you've lost your purpose, it's only because you haven't found another purpose yet."

"You must have read a lot of books in your cave," said Pierce.

"I had over a hundred, although about a third of them had pages missing or were rotting." She paused to stare at him. "Why are you smiling?"

He did the math. "You're what, twenty-three now?"

"Old enough. So are you."

"That's right, do 'old' jokes."

They both laughed. Pierce laughed harder, and harder, and finally broke down in tears. He lowered his face to the steering wheel, and sobbed. His entire body quaked with his grief. Moments later—it might have been seconds or minutes, he did not know or care—he felt her hand on his back, just below the nape of his neck. Her fingers caressed him. She was silent; he thought he would not be able to stand it if she spoke to him. He had no ears for her words of comfort. It was *not* all right. It wasn't *going to be* all right.

And then, miraculously, it was.

Moments ticked onward; his weeping subsided, and finally stilled. He lifted his head, turned it, and saw her face, inches from his. Eyes the color of polished serpentine regarded him tenderly. He found himself longing to fall into them.

A man could get lost there.
Or found.

"Talk to me," she whispered.

He found his voice. "They're gone," he breathed. "I killed all of them I could find."

Tiny furrows appeared on the bridge of her nose. "Who?"

"The . . . the presidents."

"But . . . but they're dead. Aren't they?"

Pierce sat back. Jenny set her hand gently on his thigh, and gave it a little squeeze. "Talk to me," she urged once more.

"They all had tombs, or memorials, where their bodies lay or their ashes rested in urns," he explained, his thoughts gathering momentum now that he had decided to talk. "Most had archives as well. Jenny . . . I've spent the past five years going around to each of them. I destroyed the tombs and the memorials and the archives, all I could find. I opened the urns and cast the ashes to the wind, and crushed the urns. I burned the bodies and cast away those ashes as well." He drew a huge breath, and slowly exhaled. "And now that's over. I can do no more. I'm done."

"We'll see."

He stared at her, but before he could speak, she said, "Tell me why."

"Why," he sighed. "Oh, Jenny. I've read history books, and newspaper archives, and all sorts of things, anything I could find. This used to be one country, a great country, founded on the principles of freedom for all. Little by little, we lost it—or it was taken from us. Finally we devolved into shrieking hordes, each demanding rights at the expense of others. Too many people, Jenny, too many people who kept wanting more and more. And so we fragmented, disintegrated. We balkanized. And here we are."

"But . . . the presidents?"

"They were in charge, Jenny. They symbolized this fragmentation, they allowed—even encouraged—these disparate groupings. They played people like Satan's orchestra. Now most of those folks are dead. The ones that survive, are doing just that: surviving. But it's not enough just to survive, Jenny. If there is no growth, there is only death."

She smiled. "And you want to die?"

"No." He shook his head slowly. "No, not . . . not now."

She laughed softly. "I reckon I'm to blame for that."

"Jenny," he said, and did not know what else to say to her. She was too unexpected. For someone like her to be thrust without warning into his life . . .

She broke into his anxieties. "What do you want to do?" she asked.

He made a face. "I have a cave, a very safe place," he said. "I was going back there to . . ."

"To die?"

"Maybe."

"You said 'was,'" she reminded him. "And now?"

"Jenny, we just met."

"Discovery is fun. I'll try not to snore."

"I don't know whether I do," said Pierce. "Nobody's ever nudged me awake."

"If I nudge you awake, it won't be to stop your snoring."

He rolled his eyes.

"You really didn't answer my question," she pointed out.

"I'd like to start us, everyone who's willing, on the road back," he answered slowly. "If I could do anything, I think that's what I would do."

"It's said that a journey of a thousand miles begins with a single step," she pointed out. "Maybe . . . the recovery of a nation begins with two people."

Pierce shook his head. "What can two people do?"

"Help others; isn't that what governments are supposed to do?"

"But we're not a government," he argued. "I wouldn't even want to be; we're just two people."

"So far. But I didn't mean government-type help. I meant helping folks. Like . . . okay, maybe they need a school. We can encourage them to build one; help them build it, even."

"And . . . teachers?

"We have to start somewhere. Parents can teach."

Pierce sighed. "And I suppose I could donate some of my library."

Her eyes brightened. "You have a library?"

"I've salvaged all the books I can," he said. "One time, I came across one of those used book stores that hadn't been ransacked yet. I made five trips, that time."

"You have a library," Jenny breathed. Her face saddened. "I don't even know your name."

"Jeremy Pierce."

"Jerry and Jenny," she said. "*Ad astra!*" Now her eyes matched the smile on her lips. "And now?"

"To Aunt Maude's, of course."

"Oh?"

"I'm hungry," he said. "Aren't you?"

"Oh! And then?"

"Then we go home, and you get to browse my library."

Now her smile became a veil over a secret. "I think the library will have to wait a little while."

Held Over Indefinitely
G. O. Clark

Within the bombed out city,
surrounded on all sides by the
brick and mortar rubble of lives
once spent in everyday routines,
and the metal and rubber corpses
of the wheeled American dream,

the old art deco movie theater
still stands, seemingly untouched
by the alien rain of midnight death,
their fiery projectiles, each with an
untranslatable hieroglyphic greeting,
like WW II bombs in the past,

its movie theater marquee
silently stating in bold red letters,
H. G. Wells' War Of The Worlds,
In Color by Technicolor, limited
engagement, bargain matinees daily;
snack bar popcorn machine still
full of moldy, green death.

A Wolf to Guard the Door
By Tyree Campbell

Mobs rule!

Societies around the globe have fallen apart, as more things go wrong than can be counted. Furious mobs riot, loot, torch, and slaughter. Others quietly hoard and hide, and pray. Communications function intermittently. Electromagnetic pulses damage electronics and render many vehicles useless. Soldiers and police leave their jobs to spend the last moments with their families.

One small and desperate group from the U.S. heads for the sparsely-populated and undesirable Pyrenees, hoping to be left alone. But their animosities make them a microcosm of society's breakdown. Blake's wife was butchered by Muslims. Nouh, a Boston cabbie, is a Muslim. Nollaig has just given birth and slows the group's progress. Jameela hates white folks. Addison Temple thinks he should be in charge because he has money. Tonya doesn't care for men. Miller Sinclair, an ex-Marine, is running out of patience, and she has a loaded pistol. Adriana is a Romani, her people driven out by the French. And teenager Derek Post is oblivious to everything but his GameBoy.

They've all crowded into Blake's SUV. Maybe the onrushing tsunami won't reach them. Maybe their vehicle won't run out of gas. Maybe they'll make it to the mountains.

This is the way the world ends…and might begin again…if they don't kill each other first.

https://www.hiraethsffh.com/product-page/a-wolf-to-guard-the-door-by-tyree-campbell

Looking Down To Look Up
Joseph Farley

In the 16th year of the lockdown we ran out of corpses to eat.

We had run out of bullets, canned goods, batteries, gasoline and most other things long before then.

Foraging continued to be allowed during daylight so long as the populace wore rags to cover faces, and wrapped the rest of their bodies with some kind of covering. Of course there's the social distancing, two meters or more between individuals.

Resurgent bears and wolves claimed some foragers, but not that many. Most disappearances were rumored to be at the hands of the government, rebels, gangs, or the hungry. As long as it was no one you knew, the losses could be ignored.

After CoVid 19 we had thought we would be better prepared for pandemics, but the new plague was much worse than anyone could have anticipated. There were many more dead, and the rules imposed for public safety were stricter and much more inconvenient. Violation of the rules often lead to imprisonment or execution, with execution increasing in popularity after food supplies ran low.

No vaccines worked. No old medicines, herbs or magic rights.

We all watched the breakdown of society. The deaths of doctors, nurses and other medical professionals who tried to help the sick and dying. Later, anyone with EMT experience was considered invaluable. Even former Boy Scouts with First Aid badges were pressed into service they never could have envisioned.

The medical system. The food distribution system. The economy. All shattered.

The police were merged with the military. They got better rations. They earned it by putting their lives on the line against rioters, outlaws, people that broke the rules. Those in power did not always show their appreciation, but even they knew that it was that thin line, ever growing thinner, of men and women armed and in uniform (at least at first – before it became so hard to manufacture and distribute uniforms) who stood between them and the gallows or dining table.

Not all rebels were violent. They shouted, "Freedom," refused to wear masks, stay home or keep distance. They were a danger to others and treated as such. The other rebels, the armed ones, had long believed that the world would end in chaos. They added to the chaos. Many rebels, peaceful and not so, were hunted down. But others survived, living in the deserts, the mountains, the expanding forests, both the old forests and the new ones that sprouted where abandoned corporate campuses, malls, universities, and towns once stood. Wild animals and rebels made these areas unsafe for all but best of troops.

The rebels did not care if most of their numbers died from disease. They believed in their gods, or their genes, or the process of natural selection. So they died. Then, after a period of years, they stopped dying so much. Their numbers are said to be increasing. But they are no longer the same as us. They're different. And all, even if immune themselves, are carriers.

We still manage to have elections, but it is uncertain who counts the ballots or how they are counted. Politics was always a mystery to me, more so now. There are rumors. There are always rumors. Factions, intrigue, murders. But how is that any different than what came before? It is only a matter of degree.

I voted in the last election. There was one candidate who stood out, one who offered real hope, a vision for the future. I voted for him. So did everyone else I know.

President Morlock delivered on his promise of jobs. Anyone willing to work found employment digging tunnels and building the rail system designed to carry the population underground. In the new planned cities, a half a mile or more below the surface, away from the contaminated air, we will start over. We will create a new and better civilization, abandoning the worst of what we were, keeping only the best.

Today I shall begin the descent, the journey into darkness. The president is right. That is the only way. You cannot reach heaven without the harrowing. After what we have been through, there can only be good to come.

The Ten Plagues
(Modern Day Edition)
Josh Schlossberg

"Let my people go, that they may serve me in the wilderness."
-*Exodus 7:16*

1. "All the waters that were in the river were turned to blood."

NORILSK, RUSSIA: It was still dark and chilly outside when Grigor went quietly, giddily, out of the house, fishing rod in hand. Buttoning his overcoat, he strolled through the meadow, tall dewy grass wetting his pantlegs and sneakers.

At eleven years old, he'd already caught dozens of bass in the river. But with his brand-new lure—a bright green minnow with red eyes—he'd gotten yesterday for a birthday present, Grigor had no doubt he'd catch his biggest yet. He smiled at the rim of an orange sun rising in the east. Soon the shallows would warm, and the bass would rise from the river bottom to feed.

As the dim sky blued, the factory, as always, sat on the hill above town, puffing white smoke from its stack. A light breeze carried the familiar stink of rotten eggs. But instead of wrinkling his nose like he used to do as a small boy, Grigor waved, as his mother had taught him.

Grigor knew full well that his father, hard at work in the factory, couldn't see him. But his mother said it was a good way for the boy to remind himself that the plume, nasty as it smelled, meant the factory was still open. Which meant money to pay for his clothes and shoes. Meat and vegetables on the table. Their clean and cozy house. His toys. The fishing rod he held in his numb hand that morning.

Grigor tried to remember all that as he crunched through the pine duff under the dark trees down to the river, the rotten egg smell hanging in the air. If anything, as the path sloped out from the trees towards the gurgle of water, the smell only got stronger.

Below, as always, the wide flowing river stretched out like ribbon candy. But this time, something was different. The entire waterway, from bank to bank, from the sharp curve upstream to the slight bend downstream, flowed blood red. And stunk of rotten eggs.

Grigor dropped the rod from his hand as one bass after another rose to the surface of the water. Not to feed, but with white bellies, floating.

2. "And the frogs came up and covered the land."

BATCHELOR, NORTHERN TERRITORY, AUSTRALIA: Tahnee pulled her sedan into the empty dirt lot in front of the brick veterinary office as the sun rose over the eucalyptus. Gingerly, she stepped around the dozens of fat hopping toads on her way to the front door and got the keys from her pocket.

A pickup truck rolled off the road and pulled to a halt at the edge of the lot. The office didn't officially open for another half hour, but it wasn't unusual for a worried pet owner to show up early with a sick dog or cat. And, as always, Tahnee would do her best to help.

A very old wiry man got out, leather hat crammed low over thin white hair, flannel shirt, dungarees, and leather boots coated in red dust. Rancher, probably. Tahnee waited for him to open the truck's passenger door to let out some sheepdog, but he just stood there looking at her.

A little nervous to be alone with this strange man—Oliver, her fellow vet tech was running late, per usual—Tahnee slid the key into the lock and turned it. But it wouldn't budge.

"Need you to look at something," the man said in a voice dry as January in the Outback.

The last words she wanted to hear. If she turned around, Tahnee knew the old man would have his pants down around his ankles.

"Sorry, not open yet," Tahnee said, finally realizing she'd been turning the key the wrong way. The lock snicked, and she pulled open the front door in a hurry.

"Thought you might know what this here critter is," the rancher said.

Unable to resist, Tahnee risked a peek. The old man was leaning over the bed of his pickup, staring at something. She weighed the risks. So long as she stayed out of arm's reach, the octogenarian couldn't hurt her. And even if he grabbed her, she had at least thirty pounds on him.

Duty and curiosity getting the better of her, Tahnee walked over, spiking the office key between two knuckles, just in case. Her fear, as she walked over, was that nothing would be in the truck. Holding her breath, heart pounding, keeping the man in her peripheral, she peered into the bed. It wasn't empty.

A layperson would've described it as a pointy-nosed brown squirrel with white spots and skinny tail. But Tahnee knew what it was right away.

"Where did you find it?" Tahnee hoped the man hadn't killed the animal himself. If he had, she'd need to report him.

"In the bush. Never seen nothing like it." The man took off his hat, as if in reverence, which he used to shoo away a fly. "Know what it is?"

"Northern quoll." One of the continent's many carnivorous marsupials. And this one was a near perfect specimen, plump with glossy fur. Tahnee leaned over the bed to lift it up. It barely weighed a pound, its fur feather-soft, flesh cold as dirt.

"What killed it?" the rancher asked, hat back on head again.

"Let's find out," Tahnee said.

They went inside the lobby of the office, Tahnee turning on the lights as they passed through a door into the exam room. She gently set the quoll on the metal table, where, an hour from now, she'd be injecting a border collie with its parvo booster, diagnosing a tabby with seizures, and giving a golden-tailed gecko its annual checkup. She washed her hands in the sink, dried them on a paper towel, and slipped on latex gloves, the rancher watching all the while with pale eagle eyes.

Tahnee palpated the quoll from head to tail, down each leg. Not a broken bone she could find. So, it hadn't been run over.

She opened its mouth. Pink tongue, sharp white teeth with large carnivores, it was probably little more than a yearling, which meant it hadn't died of old age. And it looked healthy, so not an infection. But wait—something down its throat.

Tahnee squinted into the dark of the animal's esophagus. A six-toed foot poking out. She got a pair of tweezers, grabbed hold, and tugged. Out came a long thick warty leg. And then the rest of the fat, dead *Bufo marinus*. Cane toad.

It had only taken a few decades for the invasive species, brought in by sugar cane farmers in the nineteen thirties to eat beetles, to overrun her homeland. Since then, it had decimated the native amphibians. And as if that wasn't bad enough, snakes and lizards found the toad delicious, only to quickly die from its toxin. Which thinned their populations, leading to a boom of rats which, ironically, ate up the very crops the toad was supposed to save.

"That what killed it?" the rancher asked in a hushed voice.

Tahnee nodded. Not just this quoll, but so many across the continent that they were now at the verge of extinction, officially classified as an endangered species.

With a thumb, Tahnee pressed down on one of the bulging sacs behind the toad's staring golden eyes. A white film seeped out.

"Buggers got my dog, too, then," the rancher whispered.

Tahnee set the toad down on the table beside the quoll. "I'm sorry," she said. But the rancher had already left.

The front door slammed shut. Tahnee waited for the sound of the pickup's engine to turn over. Instead, a grunting.

She looked out the window to the parking lot. The rancher was stomping the dirt with the heel of his leather boots, as if putting out tiny fires. Crushing toads.

An act of cruelty, as the toads were living creatures, felt pain, and hadn't asked to be imported from their home range. Tahnee was paid to protect animals.

She sighed. But then again, these newcomers were wiping out those that had always been there, wildlife that kept the ecosystem—upon which all life depended—functioning.

Tahnee wasn't sure whether to go out there to chase off the rancher or help him.

She ended up standing there watching him squash toads. Until maybe five minutes later, after barely having made a dent in the scores of hopping invaders, the old man shuffled back to his pickup, started it up, and sped off down the road in a rooster tail of dust.

3. "So there were lice upon man, and upon beast."

MILLBROOK, NEW YORK: Marcus picked up a navel orange from the grocery store display and sniffed it to make sure it was ripe. Feeling hot, he set it back down. Laid a wrist against his forehead and, sure enough, he was burning up. Probably that darned bug going around.

Not wanting to spread the virus to the other shoppers, he put the orange he'd touched in a plastic bag, dropped it in his cart, and went to the bathroom to wash his hands.

Splashing his flushed face with cold water from the sink, Marcus shook his head at the irony of going on a trip to the Adirondacks with Amy, his fiancée, for the sole purpose of stress relief, only to come back sick.

Still, it was worth a few sniffles for all the swimming, sailing, and rounds of golf they'd enjoyed at the resort. Of course, he'd been surprised by how civilized the area was now, the dense forests he'd hiked in during summer camp cleared for suburban housing developments. But those late night "workouts" in the room had more than made up for all that.

Marcus yanked a paper towel from the dispenser and patted his forehead dry. Some water had run down his neck, so he wiped that, too. Then blinked a few times at the mirror. A pink blotch on the side of his neck.

Marcus pulled back the collar of his T-shirt to expose the rest of his neck. The pink rash was the size of a fist, surrounded by a circle of white flesh followed by another ring of pink. Like a bullseye.

Marcus squinted. In the center of the red spot, a tiny black pinprick like a poppy seed. He leaned closer to the mirror, breath fogging it, which he cleared away with the towel.

The poppy seed had legs. He gasped, horrified.

Not a seed but a deer tick.

4. "There came a grievous swarm of flies."

ABUJA, NIGERIA: It hurt so much just lying there in bed in the delivery room. The lights above a row of blinding suns. The stink of antiseptic stinging the inside of Ileara's nostrils.

But Okoro, her beloved, smiled with deep brown eyes over his surgical mask, and she knew everything would be okay.

Though they still hadn't picked a name. Mostly because they didn't know—hadn't wanted to—if it was a boy or a girl. The newlyweds had a few contenders, of course, but couldn't settle on one. Ileara's choice for a boy was Uche. Orisa, if a girl. Okoro's were Enofe and Chinara.

At seven months pregnant, Ileara figured they had plenty of time to figure it out. But then, an hour ago, while making a fresh batch of pepper soup, her water broke. Their baby was coming.

"Almost there," the blue-gowned doctor said from between Ileara's feet hanging in the stirrups.

But Ileara didn't *want* to be almost there. It was too soon. They didn't even have a name! How could she have a baby without a name?

"Now, push!" the doctor said.

With no other way out, Ileara took a breath and gave it her all. The pain was awful, at the brink of where unbearable crossed over to impossible. And then, finally, it was over.

She closed her eyes, her labor of love complete.

But other than the hum of some machine and a muffled announcement from the P.A. in the hall, it was quiet. Too quiet. The baby should be crying.

Ileara opened her eyes. And from Okoro's glazed stare, she knew their baby was dead.

Then a cry! And a second! Loud as the dickens from what could only be strong, healthy lungs!

Ileara held out her arms, but the nurse wouldn't look at her. "May I hold my baby now?"

The baby cried and cried. It needed its mother! "I want my baby!" Ileara shouted.

Finally, the nurse brought over the blanket-wrapped bundle and gently set it in Ileara's arms. Ileara held the warm, squirming, screeching newborn to her bare breast. And loosened the blanket from around the baby's head.

Ileara's breath caught. The head. A wet mop of hair, but something was wrong with the head. Ileara blinked, hoping it was a hallucination from the pain meds.

She ran her fingers over the baby's downy skull. The forehead too low, sloped, like part of the brain was missing. Ileara felt a million miles away, yet somehow still held onto her baby, who wouldn't stop crying.

Okoro stood over her, looking at the floor. He whispered something like *Rita* or maybe *Shira*. New names he'd chosen? Did that mean it was a girl?

He said it again. It was not the baby's name.

"Zika," he mumbled.

5. "A very grievous murrain."

UMATILLA NATIONAL FOREST, OREGON: The sun shone high in the sky, its light filtering greenly through tall cedars, last night's snow sloughing off lacy branches. Thirteen-year-old Harlan, sitting with his back propped against a fat old growth trunk, wrapped in a wool blanket against the mild chill, popped the last chunk of jerky in his mouth and chewed the salty, savory toughness.

In a few hours Sammy, his older brother, would be waiting for him at the turnout with his pickup. After a total of five hunting trips this fall, Harlan still hadn't harvested so much as a squirrel. So, two days before, he'd set off on his own into the national forest with nothing but his father's rifle, last season's jerky, bottle of water, and blanket.

But deer and elk avoided Harlan like the plague, as they had all season, and it appeared he was destined to return home empty handed and disgraced yet again. The fact that it was already early December—the time for the wintering of the herds—meant it was his last chance this year.

His usual tack of sitting quietly for hours, imagining himself invisible, had clearly failed him. In one motion, Harlan threw off the blanket and rose to his feet. Rifle in hand, he wandered into a grove of massive Douglas fir, eyes on the soft melting snow in front of him, ears pricked for the telltale snap of a twig. Finally, a pair of heart-shaped hoofprints set his heart athump, but on closer inspection they were melted, swollen...old.

He moved on deeper into the forest, yet the snow was smooth as a bank of clouds. Bladder full, he unbuttoned his pants to take a whizz. And that's when he saw the tracks. He crouched to touch them with his bare fingers. Deep and sharp in the snow, as if the animal had passed by moments before.

With only a few hours before sundown, he hurried on. And before very long, he found the deer.

From behind it looked small. But it was either this doe or none at all. Swiftly, smoothly, silently, Harlan unclicked the safety, raised the rifle stock to his shoulder, and took aim.

As if in slow motion, the deer turned to face Harlan, its black nostrils pulsing to take in his scent. He expected it to bolt, but it didn't.

Harlan took in a breath through his nose, sighted at the left center of the animal's chest, and then slowly exhaled through his mouth as he squeezed the trigger.

The loud shot flew straight and true into the doe's chest. Not a second later, the animal dropped onto its side and lay still on the snow. The fire of victory flared inside Harlan, knowing he could finally face his brother—and himself—again.

Harlan slid the buck knife from its sheath and sprinted over in case his quarry tried to run. But it hadn't moved an inch, its eyes glazed open with death's one-thousand-foot stare. A one-inch diameter hole where the round had found the creature's heart, dripping blood making a cherry slushie in the snow.

Yet Harlan's excitement went out like a campfire in a downpour. During the time of year where a deer should be fat from summer and fall's gorging, not only wasn't it much larger than a fawn, it was bony, almost shrunken—like a dried plum—as if it had already gone through a very hard winter.

Disappointed as he was, Harlan took comfort in the fact that it had clearly been the animal's time. Much better to do as the wolves and cougars did by taking weak ones like this than robbing a herd of its biggest buck, who would otherwise go on to sire more like him come spring.

But this little doe, hide patchy and worn, ribs jutting, didn't look old. Harlan's stomach soured as he recalled the "wasting" sickness among the herds of deer, elk, and moose. Supposedly, white men had started it years ago with their deer farms, and then their government had spread it into the wild with its feedgrounds.

But this sickness wasn't supposed to hurt people. And speaking of wasting, it would be wrong to simply leave the meat to rot.

Harlan shifted the deer onto its back and, with his blade, slit the hide and skin from just below its gaunt sternum down to its taut belly. It took him about a half hour to field dress the animal, removing the organs and leaving them steaming on the snow for the ravens and coyotes.

As the sun sunk low through the screen of cedars, Harlan hoisted the carcass on his back and trudged out through the snow to the road.

6. "It became a boil breaking forth with blains upon man."

PUNTARENAS, COSTA RICA: Lucia stood over the sink in her brightly lit bathroom. Holding her breath, she pulled the bandage off the inside of her forearm. Then sighed in dismay. Not only hadn't the itchy quarter-sized bloody wound healed, it was leaking yellow pus.

At first, she'd thought it was a spider bite. Lord knew there were enough of those things crawling around town. But Dr. Cruz had told her it was probably just a run of the mill staph infection, and if she applied over-the-counter antibiotic cream it would probably heal within a week.

Well, a week later, things were only getting worse, and it was all Lucia could do to keep from scratching her arm off. She picked up the phone and dialed the doctor. Luckily, he had a last-minute cancelation if she could make it in before the office closed in an hour.

She left her apartment and went down the stairs into the quiet street to wait for the bus. It came, she found a seat up front, and was at the doctor in ten minutes.

Lucia sat on crinkly butcher paper on the examination table in the rubbing alcohol-scented back room and peeled off the bandage.

Dr. Cruz took a quick look, deep lines creasing the sides of his caramel eyes. He didn't beat around the bush. "There's only so much we can do."

Lucia almost laughed, thinking it was a joke—the idea that she was about to die from a small sore on her arm. But the doctor didn't smile.

Lucia's chest got tight, and she felt faint.

Clearly picking up on her discomfort, Cruz followed up quickly, "As in, it'll probably clear up on its own."

Coming back to herself, Lucia finally did laugh, in relief. "Oh, for a second there, I thought—"

"But you're not out of the woods yet." Cruz rubbed his gloved hands together. "I'll need a sample, but I'm pretty sure it's MRSA."

Lucia had heard the name before but was foggy on the details. "I thought it was staph."

"It *is* staph. Methicillin-resistant Staphylococcus aureus." Cruz went into a cabinet and rooted around. Came back out with a small petri dish and long cotton swab and set the dish down on the metal table. "But this kind doesn't respond well to the antibiotics we've been using. Overusing. Hell, abusing."

Her head was swimming with the diagnosis. "So why not new antibiotics?"

"We've done that, and we'll do it again." He gently grasped her wrist. "But that's also how more strains keep evolving. Stronger and stronger."

Lucia was done with the science lesson. She flexed her forearm. "Am I going to be okay?"

"Like I said, most cases clear up," he said.

Lucia took in a sharp breath as he wiped the tip of the swab across the center of her aching wet wound.

"And if not?" Electric panic flooded her system. "Could I die from this?"

"I didn't say that." Dr. Cruz rubbed the cotton in the petri dish and closed it up with a snap.

"But you didn't *not* say that," Lucia said.

The doctor sighed as he got a fresh bandage from a drawer. "Let's just say it's highly, highly unlikely."

Lucia's whirring brain wasn't about to let him off that easy. "But not impossible?"

Dr. Cruz didn't answer as he applied the bandage.

7. "Thunder and hail, and the fire ran along upon the ground."

SUPERIOR, COLORADO: The hailstorm was the first drop of precipitation in almost two months. Sure, the Front Range didn't often see real snow until January. But this December, things had been dry as a bone.

Randy's Prius was parked in the garage, so he didn't have to worry about dents. He just stood in his living room of his townhome watching through the big picture window as ice pellets dropped from slate grey clouds to pelt his neighbors' two giant SUVs and speckle the shared driveway.

Three minutes later it was over and done, and a bright late afternoon sun stripped the clouds from a denim blue sky. Randy went into the marble and chrome kitchen to brew a cup of green tea. And had just sat down to scan the paper when the picture window rattled in its frame.

The wind had picked up something fierce after the hailstorm and was rushing down from Boulder's famous red rock Flatirons like a sea gale. Randy shrugged and went back to the paper; living where the mountains met the high prairie meant heavy winds, sometimes gusts up to a hundred miles an hour. That's why there was the small, spider web crack in the upper right-hand corner of the window, something he'd have to repair this spring before it got so bad he'd need to replace the whole thing.

The whistling picked up while he read, buffeting the townhouse like a ship in the middle of the stormy Atlantic. Tea drained, he rinsed the mug, set it in the sink, and strolled over to the window. The grey cloud was back. Another hailstorm?

Randy went to the front door but, incredibly, wasn't able to pull it open. That's how hard the wind was blowing. When the gust died, he yanked the door back so fast it almost hit him in the nose, the knob smashing a dent in the wall plaster.

The wind gave him a stiff shove in the chest as it cut across his suburban front yard, whipping up sticks and scraps of plastic, swaying the manicured bushes bordering the driveway. The grey cloud was low in the sky, but it wasn't hail. It was smoke.

The spicy tang in the air was typical, what with the number of woodstoves in the densely packed neighborhood. With Randy's asthma, the last thing he needed was to suck down a bunch of particulates. So he shut the door, locked it, and plopped down on the couch to read his spy novel.

The wind screamed, but one sound was louder: his neighbor's TV. The middle-aged couple and their twentysomething daughter had moved in six months ago, and though they all had jobs, someone always seemed to be home blaring reality shows or blockbuster action films, from nine a.m. until eleven p.m.

Annoying as it was, Randy hadn't bothered talking to them, knowing how unwilling people were to change their precious habits, how even bringing up such things only won you enemies. Instead, he'd ordered a top-of-the-line white noise machine along with a pair of noise canceling headphones. When he wanted some peace and quiet, he conjured up his forcefield of silence.

Randy slipped on his headphones, plugged them into the little black box, spun the dial over to the crash of ocean waves, and opened his book.

The imaginary audio ocean was so immersive Randy didn't hear his phone buzz with the alert. Nor the doorbell or furious pounding.

At the end of the chapter, he got up to pee. On his way past the picture window, Randy casually glanced outside to see if things might be shaping up for a pretty sunset. And stopped short. Because the scene made no sense.

Randy blinked hard, thinking he might've nodded off while reading and was in the middle of a dream. But the shriek of the wind and the heat seeping through the cracking pane was no dream. Nor was the wave of orange flames breaking over the driveway, heading straight for him.

8. "Before them there were no such locusts as they."

BLAINE COUNTY, MONTANA: Slowly, creakily, painfully, Don knelt down on one knee to pinch up a crumb of soil from the edge of the field. More dust than dirt, it powdered between his rough fingers. He shook his head and got to his feet again, surveying his golden acres of wheat stretching out to the foothills.

Despite the new-fangled drip irrigation system he'd dumped most of his savings into, this year's yield was bound to be two-thirds of what it should. First, there'd been the floods. Then a decade-long drought, all but drying up the groundwater. And after that, the leaf rust and stem rot. As his father used to say when he ran the farm, if it wasn't one damn thing, it was another.

Down by the dry wash, a peach of a sun dipped low over the cottonwoods. Don took off his sweaty ball cap and itched his stubbly scalp. If he hadn't sold Bucky, his old gelding, he might've had half a notion to ride off into that there sunset. Instead, he wandered into the field, parting the amber waves of grain like a dusty Moses.

It wasn't like he'd ever expected Zachary to take over for him. Farming was no life for a boy with that one's restlessness and hunger. Still, it hurt to see the indifference —the scorn, even—for the land on which his son had been born and raised. The land, handed down for three generations, that Don had worked for nigh on thirty years to sustain them all.

He walked on between the rows, crushing the clods beneath his bootheels.

And would it kill the kid to visit? Shoot, since Myrtle's passing, Zachary had made the trip back from New York, what, three times? Whether it was table manners or politics, they didn't see eye to eye on much, but Don always loved his son deeply and figured the current went both ways. But just like the well he'd dug back in ought-six, seemed that'd dried up, too.

Just before dark, with only a few coyote yips to keep him company, Don found himself in the dead center of his acreage.

A chittering. He froze. It'd be just his luck to get bit by a rattler. But it was too high-pitched for that. And this was a chorus, no lone voice. He sniffed a laugh. Just crickets.

For no reason at all, Don felt drawn to the sound and ambled on. Then sucked in a dry breath. The closer he got, the more chewed up the wheat spikes. Until they were all stem and leaf, and in some cases, just stem. A few big crickets hopped out from under his boots, as the chirring got louder.

Here, the wheat was black. But not from mold.

Don had known they were coming. Decimating crops across five western states, they'd been the last nail in the coffin for the handful of family farms still hanging on. He'd even heard tell that they'd made it over the mountains, just hadn't let himself think about it much, knowing there wasn't much he could do, anyway. Or maybe hoping he'd be gone before they got there.

Not crickets, of course, but grasshoppers. Swarms of them massing on the wheat, chewing out the chaffy heart of the land, of the man himself.

9. "And there was a thick darkness in all the land."

HENGSHUI, CHINA: Xiang reached for the shampoo bottle as the showerhead spurted the last of its lukewarm water against her chest. WASH, RINSE, REPEAT, the label read. She popped the cap and squeezed the bottle, but nothing came out.

Get up. Drive to work. Stare at the computer.

Drive home. Stare at the TV. Go to sleep.

Wash. Rinse. Repeat.

Sighing, Xiang unscrewed the cap, held it under the now cold water, and put the cap back on. Shook the bottle, popped the cap again, and dumped the slimy dregs over her head.

Exhausted from the night's fitful sleep, Xiang may have let a few tears trickle down her face. Or maybe it was just the shower. Machines did everything for her—entertainment, shopping, socializing—so why not the crying, too?

Out of the shower. Dried, primped, and dressed. Hurrying from her tiny apartment to squeeze into the even smaller crowded elevator. Per usual, she didn't recognize any of the faces. And, all staring straight ahead, none appeared to recognize hers.

Standing before the automatically revolving glass doors, Xiang got her mask out of her pocket, slipped it on her face, and fitted it tightly around the bridge of her nose. Waiting for a break in the throng, she darted into her own compartment and rushed through like a hamster on its wheel before being spat out onto the sidewalk and the chaotic blare of engine and horn.

One good thing about the pandemic was she'd gotten used to the mask. But at least then she'd been able to walk safely through the park, or the occasional empty sidewalk, without it. These days, she couldn't recall a time when she'd set foot outside not wearing one.

At 8:07, the sun had been up for nearly two hours. But the city streets, junk-filled canyons cutting through high rise cliffs, were like dusk, the thick yellow haze making it impossible to see more than a hundred feet in any direction. Less than a decade ago, the air had been fine, but every year since then, it had gotten worse. And now, as bad as it was, everyone just took it for granted.

Xiang's eyes stung as she got carried along the packed sidewalk to where her car was parked in the overflowing lot. She got in, took off her mask, cranked the air conditioner, and veered into the standstill traffic, tailpipe feeding the cloud.

10. "All the firstborn in the land shall die."

SANDY SPRINGS, GEORGIA: Mom and Dad had finally gone upstairs to bed, thank God. Finally, with no one breathing down his neck, watching his every move, Ethan could feel at home. He plopped down on the couch in the dark living room, put his sneakers up on the ottoman, and turned on the TV.

Of course, it *was* Ethan's home. Always had been. And that was the problem.

At thirty-nine, society insisted he have a job, wife, children, house of his own. Instead, he'd skipped all that and went straight into early retirement. But without the companionship. Or the satisfaction of having contributed something to the world. Or the money to support himself.

On the widescreen TV, taking up a third-of the wall, an obese elderly woman waddled between teetering piles of junk—magazines, heaps of clothing, cardboard boxes—mewling cat twining between her slippered feet. Having seen this episode before, Ethan switched the channel to some infomercial for hair growth—a product he'd tried that hadn't worked.

He took a long pull from his can of warm syrupy root beer.

The worst part was that instead of Ethan taking care of his parents in their twilight years, they were taking care of him. It was pathetic, and not an hour passed without him drowning in the shame of it all.

Up until a few years ago, Ethan had hoped a woman might've been the way out of his Peter Pan nightmare. But after thousands of swipes, scores of ghosted messages, and a handful of awkward dates, he'd decided the certain pain of dating to be far greater than the infinitesimal chance of actual connection and had deleted all the apps.

More out of boredom than desire, Ethan switched off the TV, clomped down to the moldy, half-finished basement, sat in the video game chair at the desk, and flipped open his laptop. He pulled up the bookmarked website and, after listening a few seconds to make sure the coast was clear, clicked on the suggested video.

A nude, ninety-pound bottle blonde with a spray tan did jumping jacks in an empty gym, balloon breasts almost smacking her chin. But porn's insincerity had long ago ceased to get Ethan's juices flowing, and he angrily slammed the laptop shut.

Scanning the dim basement in listless desperation, his gaze fell on the acoustic guitar leaning against the cinderblock wall in the corner. Even though he'd stopped performing, the instrument still helped pass the time. He went over and picked it up. But he'd forgotten that two of the strings were broken. And he hadn't bought any new ones.

Shaking his head at his laziness, he set it back down hard, the *bong* of it hitting the wall the only music he'd made in weeks.

All that was left was the medicine. Sure, doctors insisted his fractured patella had healed. But it still hurt. Or at least that's what Ethan told himself every time his prescription ran out.

With a sigh, he looked out the single tiny dusty street-level window, the streetlamp shining bright yellow on the big spruce tree out front.

Sometimes a man needed his solace. But these days, the medicine didn't even work that well. The bliss of those first few times had proven impossible to recreate, always just out of reach, like the beach to a swimmer caught in a rip tide.

And unlike pot, it didn't make things funnier. Unlike mushrooms, it didn't peel away the layers to the thrumming mysteries of life. Unlike MDMA, it didn't fire up his physical senses. And unlike booze, it didn't make him jolly. But now that the training wheels had come off the bike, there was no going back.

A car drove past, stinging Ethan's eyes in the sweep of its headlights. He closed them. And kept them closed.

Maybe he didn't deserve to feel better, this worthless husk of a man that he was, this drain on his parents, on the system itself. It had been a mistake for him to be born, after all, and from what society was telling him, nothing he did could ever absolve him.

The medicine did, however, numb him. Which was good enough. Or, at least, had been.

He opened his eyes, the spruce tree still there. The opposite of his friends who had, one by one, started drifting away like autumn leaves. And then, like a killing frost, all at once.

But it wasn't people Ethan missed the most. It was the forest. Hiking the never-ending miles of trail, muscles working, blood pumping, thoughts flowing. It had never felt like more than recreation at the time, but now he realized his hikes in the unpeopled wilds were when he'd felt most connected to the world. Most alive. Most himself.

The nearest hiking trail was only a twenty-minute drive, but after the accident he'd been nervous to get behind the wheel. And it was obviously too late in the night to ask his parents for a ride, something he'd never do during the day, anyway.

He supposed he could call a cab. Have the guy drive him out there and wait as he went for a short stroll with his headlamp. Ethan smiled at the glimmer of hope. It wouldn't be much, but it would be something. And, in time, he could build back his strength, and maybe, with it, his confidence.

Ethan patted his pocket for his phone, but he'd left it all the way upstairs. Fuck.

Truth was, even if he did get out on the trail, he wouldn't make it more than a half mile without wheezing, thanks to the lingering effects of last year's "mild" case of COVID. Plus, he was fat, now. Yes, the kid they used to call "Thin Ethan" in high school was now too fat to go for a goddamn walk.

The root beer finally sludging its way down to his bladder, he went to the bathroom and snapped on the one working bulb over the medicine chest above the sink. As always, he dribbled piss over the rim and the floor. As always, he didn't bother cleaning it up.

There was, of course, one way for Ethan to escape his suburban prison, to return to the wild nature he loved, the source from which he—everything—had come. He'd put off the trip for a while. Yet with the first sense of resolve he'd felt in years, he knew it was finally time.

Ethan opened the medicine chest, careful not to look at himself in the cracked, smudged mirror. Got out the translucent orange bottle and unscrewed the lid. Dumped the pills in his palm and counted them out.

One. Two. Three. All the way to ten.

When the Mushrooms Come
By Francis W. Alexander

The Atomic Age brought with it many wonders and great strides forward. It also brought nuclear war. We often forget how many nuclear warheads are still scattered about our world, and how many countries are still trying to make their own. What would happen to ordinary people if one fell without warning? Follow along in the lives of different people as they move through the drop of a nuclear bomb – before, during, and after the fall. See their lives before the flash, their reactions when the mushroom cloud rises, and how the survivors struggle on.

https://www.hiraethsffh.com/product-page/when-the-mushrooms-come-by-francis-w-alexander

Movie Review: Leave the World Behind

Lee Clark Zumpe

'Leave the World Behind' offers an ominous take on societal collapse.

Hear me out: Sometimes it feels like society is breaking down in front of us. The harbingers of this decline are manifest in a growing disregard for the foundations of democracy, in the inability to differentiate between personal opinion and scientific fact, in a sociopathic willingness to ignore laws, and in the tendency to put one's own selfish interests above those of the community as a whole.

Sometimes it feels like the world is teetering on the edge of a cliff, with civilization poised to collapse under the combined pressure of evolving challenges and potential catastrophes — everything from resource depletion, economic meltdown, and ecosystem degradation to sociopolitical disintegration, emerging pandemic threats, and nuclear war. Sometimes it feels like we are stumbling blindly — drunkenly — toward the precipice, eager to hurl ourselves into the abyss.

Sometimes I wonder if there's any hope we'll recover our collective humanity.

"Leave the World Behind," an apocalyptic thriller, delves into the psychological and sociological effects of experiencing a series of calamitous events. Written and directed by Sam Esmail, the film is based on the 2020 novel of the same name by Rumaan Alam. Following a limited theatrical release on Nov. 22, "Leave the World Behind" began streaming Dec. 8 on Netflix.

Populated by unlikable, antisocial characters forced to work in partnership and pool resources during an unfolding crisis, the film is as exasperating as it is disturbing. Esmail maintains an overwhelming tone of tension and anxiety, plunging the attentive viewer into a fog of uncertainty and trepidation. Watching "Leave the World Behind" is stressful. It is a demanding, thought-provoking story that is sometimes uncomfortable and difficult to process. Its message about interpersonal relationships, the deterioration of social conventions, and about how individuals can be easily manipulated into dehumanizing the Other is perceptive and pertinent.

The film opens in New York. Amanda Sanford (Julia Roberts) wants to get away from people. She surprises her husband Clay (Ethan Hawke) by renting a lavish home on Long Island for a weekend getaway with their kids, Archie (Charlie Evans) and Rose (Farrah Mackenzie). On the drive to the rental, Archie plays a video game while Rose continues binging the 1990s sitcom "Friends."

A relaxing day at the beach is interrupted when an oil tanker runs ashore, providing the first evidence that something is amiss.

On the first night of their impromptu vacation, two strangers — G.H. (Mahershala Ali) and his adult daughter Ruth (Myha'la Herrold) — arrive at the front door of the home. G.H. identifies himself as the owner of the house and explains that they fled the city due to a blackout. By morning, the WiFi is network is down, the television is displaying an Emergency Alert System warning message, phones are unusable and GPS devices are not operable.

Bits and pieces of information — and possibly misinformation — reach the two families, and it becomes evident that the United States is under attack. As panic sets in, friction between the homeowners and the renters surfaces, with Amanda and Ruth both voicing their opinion that in a time of crisis, there is no room for altruism. Each initially lacks any compassion for the other, and exhibits distrust and callousness.

Clay is powerless and indecisive, making empty promises to protect his family while knowing there is nothing he can do to stop what's happening. Archie and Rose are mostly frustrated by being disconnected from their digital devices and plunged into isolation. Rose — who seems far too mature and sophisticated for her age — eventually recognizes the failure of the adults to formulate a viable plan to meet their immediate needs for survival and acts accordingly.

G.H. eventually admits that he observed telltale signs that something was about to happen, but that he had put faith in government officials and in democratic institutions to keep this scenario from becoming reality. After a tense meeting with his neighbor Danny (Kevin Bacon), a survivalist, G.H. tells Clay what he believes has transpired — and suggests that they need to take shelter in an underground bunker.

Many questions are left unanswered by the film's abrupt, vague conclusion. Although some viewers may find the ending abstruse and dissatisfying, it is the lingering ambiguity that makes the film so intriguing and unsettling.

Overall, the ensemble cast delivers compelling performances, even though some character interactions seem either incongruous or unnecessary. Roberts is at her best when Amanda is at her worst: Roberts underscores the misanthropic side of the character's personality, even in the way she interacts with her husband and children. Ali's depiction of G.H. is outstanding, rendering him as a man of stolid composure, considerate nature, and considerable intellect. He has paid a hefty price for his unwillingness to perceive the seismic activity in the financial world that preceded the event.

To some degree, each character is consumed by the banal trivialities of existence. Some are addicted to media consumption, some are driven by animal instincts even when faced with an existential threat, and some are prone to lapse into apathy and inertia. Overcome by fatalism, the characters are not masters of their fate: They have been lulled into a false sense of security and are subservient to their desire for comfort and amusement.

Clearly unaware of their selfishness, these characters are mired in the callow and superficial dogma of egoism. Their epiphanies come too late, leaving them with a ringside seat from which they can watch the world fall into chaos. The film is a cautionary tale on the fragility of society, about classism and racism and other mechanisms that can be used to cause friction and disunity. It leaves the viewer to reflect upon an ominous message about where the world might be heading.

In a sense, "Leave the World Behind" is a contemporary homage to "The Monsters Are Due on Maple Street," episode 22 of the first season of "The Twilight Zone."

First broadcast in March 1960 and written by Rod Serling, that episode concludes with a similar message: "The tools of conquest do not necessarily come with bombs and explosions and fallout. There are weapons that are simply thoughts, attitudes, prejudices, to be found only in the minds of men. For the record, prejudices can kill, and suspicion can destroy. And a thoughtless, frightened search for a scapegoat has a fallout all of its own — for the children and the children yet unborn."

Lee Clark Zumpe is entertainment editor at Tampa Bay Newspapers, a Tomatometer-Approved Critic, and an author of short fiction appearing in select anthologies and magazines. Follow Lee at www.patreon.com/Haunter_of_the_Bijou.

Wearing Winter Gray
By Lee Clark Zumpe

Atmospheric poetry at its finest is found in Wearing Winter Gray. Lee Clark Zumpe sets his moods and draws forth evocative images and memories, and not a little emotion. Now and then a ray of light shines through his words, so that having created a somber mood, he punctuates it with a bit of joy. Thus it is that Wearing Winter Gray reminds us that Shiny Summer Colors are just around the corner.

Type: Poetry collection
Ordering links:
Print ($9.95): https://www.hiraethsffh.com/product-page/wearing-winter-gray-by-lee-clark-zumpe
ePub ($2.99): https://www.hiraethsffh.com/product-page/wearing-winter-gray-by-lee-clark-zumpe-2
PDF ($2.99): https://www.hiraethsffh.com/product-page/wearing-winter-gray-by-lee-clark-zumpe-1

Mother
Christopher Hivner

Moving towards the stars
in a ship built by another race
we were not conquerors
but finders of the lost

in the desert
buried for a century
once under dunes as tall as buildings
nomads found the ship

scientists, pilots, bureaucrats
decades of minds
coming and going
before we could finally fly

specialists were chosen
never to be seen again
on Earth
but to be immortalized in our history

decades of traveling
crew in and out of stasis
less and less
contact with home

now we approach the star
that provides life
to the planets of the alien system
a blue giant shining like a gem

still millions of miles
from the ship's home world
console lights flash
in dizzying color

a message is received
decoded and translated
by machines
our best minds built

To all lost ships
do not return to the home world
a contagion has taken over
our world is lost

You are all that remain
of our race
explore the universe
don't let us be forgotten

Our minds reel
at the meaning
they're all gone
a race that found us

We will never meet
in life
will never see
the alien world

In months
we finally see it
a dark sphere
trying to hide

We drift past the planet
our eyes taking in all we can
of the first world visited
outside of our solar system

As we speed into the void
we ruminate on what's happened
and send our own message back to Earth
do not forget us

Loyal Employee
Rob McMonigal

He sweeps the steps carefully, making sure not a single speck of dust remains on what they used to call the gateway to independence. Every day, he works the ancient brush across marble that's seen better days, thinking about important people who climbed up these stairs.

Clay. Both Roosevelts. Both Bushes. Gingrich, like it or not. That black guy with the funny ears who kept trying to bring the warring sides together. The granddaughter of Hillary Clinton, who finally broke the glass ceiling at the highest level. All used this path, at some point or another.

Now it was his and his alone. The city, once so vibrant, has already begun returning to its natural state, when it was a backwater swamp that no one wanted. No cars make the trek down the Avenue, though plenty are stopped in their tracks with exploded tires, shattered windows, and melted plastic alloys designed to withstand impacts unmatched by the horror visited upon them. Tourists are long gone. Mosquitoes hover, looking for the victims they've attacked in prior years, but find only his hardened skin.

He swats them ineffectively, with a bright blue handkerchief that's dampened by sweat. Figures they'd make it through this hellscape. Unlike him, they're willing survivors, though. A passing shard of newspaper nips at his heels. The only words visible are in a big, bold font:
IT'S WAR

The man kicks the paper away, preferring not to be reminded. His mind returns to the scene of his crime anyway: Watching his family die before his eyes on a cellular screen, peeling apart in the heat of the blast while he looked on, stupidly trying to remember if he'd kissed them goodbye that morning. That memory, too, vaporized in the moment his world ended.

He spits, cursing the fact that he was at work, protected like his bosses that were supposed to prevent this from ever happening.

They'd failed. He would not.

His broom shook white ash frantically into the air, dispersing the bugs around him.

It was almost comical to watch the looks on the face of the "important people" as they realized that there were maybe a few dozen people like him who weren't "essential" yet had survived the blast. Remaining supplies were finite, and how could someone as important as the Commander in Chief be expected to share his resources with a common janitor?

His employers answered this rather quickly by sealing off the "non-specialized" personnel and then opening the doors as soon as it was "safe" for them to return home. It wasn't so much a pink slip as a premature obituary.

That was okay with him; they had to live with the death of millions. He only had to deal with survivor's guilt, and even that would end when his willpower finally gives out.

The clouds refuse to move as he climbs the steps ever-higher. He knows it's not true, not exactly, but he feels the radiation seeping into his pores, bit by bit. He'll run out of canned goods soon, but unlike the others he won't try for more. Hell, maybe complications from the radiation will get him long before a lack of pork and beans do.

When the time comes, he is prepared to die. Until then, he'll keep sweeping these steps, fulfilling the job he was hired to do.

The broom makes a satisfying swoosh just as the first blisters appear on his hands.

He'll remain a loyal employee until the end.

They Came in Peace
John Darling

When the first Odd Radio Signal, or ORC as we dubbed it, was spotted down under by the Australian Square Kilometre Array Pathfinder, we were fascinated and stumped at the same time. What caused it and what it was made of were questions that captivated our imagination.

When South Africa's MeerKAT Array Pathfinder discovered four more the following week, we wondered how many more were out there.

We had no answers.

We could only make assumptions about these unknown peculiar green entities that glowed brightly against space's pitch-black background. Most of our assumptions would later prove false. Nevertheless, if we had made correct analyses of the situation, in all probability, it would have changed nothing. What played out would always play out. Humans were too insignificant to alter the cosmic ways of the universe.

Our script has been written since the beginning of time.

What theories we developed ran the gamut of the astronomical community. From space-time warps to Einstein Rings to remnants of a Super Nova, we covered everything, but in the end, we had no concrete knowledge of what ORCs were. So, we made some mistakes along the way.

Perhaps our biggest mistake came from our attempts to fit ORCs into the science we knew while not admitting that they were something beyond our current knowledge. Our impertinence caused us to miscalculate what constituted an ORC. We categorized them as arbitrary radio waves creating circles in space. Then we used our imperfect science to estimate their distance from our Solar System.

Our next mistake was misjudging their speed as they moved through infinite space. We should have been aware of this from the beginning since one day there were no ORCs to be seen, then the next day, one appeared. Shortly afterward, four more were discovered. In the next month, six more were found, and at least a dozen other spots in the blackness were suspected of being ORCs.

We know that light travels 670,616,629 miles per hour, so since we assumed that ORCs were just light beams with a mass less than a butterfly's breath, our science estimated them to be several billion light-years from Earth. Subsequently, we took our time studying them.

We presumed that they would not enter our Solar System for centuries to come, even though they seemed to be growing at a worrying rate.

At least we thought they were growing. That was another one of our mistakes.

Without actual data about how they were created and what they were made of, there was no way for us to accurately measure their distance from our planet. We could only guess. The truth is that they were not growing as we thought.

ORCs were just moving closer to Earth.

Before men of science realized that their growth was merely an optical illusion, strange things began happening on Moon Base Icarus, located on the far side of the moon.

Icarus was the last place any member of the U.S. Space Force wanted to be posted. Rotations were short, three months, then the entire crew was replaced. Any longer stays at Icarus were found to cause severe mental disorders due to its isolation and dimness due to its lack of earthshine.

I was the Principal Astrobiologist stationed in Moon Base Copernicus on the lighter side. One of my colleagues of the same discipline lived in Icarus. We talked daily, often for hours. So, when the base stopped transmitting, we were all concerned.

More so since their last transmission to Copernicus was very disturbing.

Shortly before they went to total radio silence, they reported a quickly-repaired breach in an airlock in a small storage facility on the far side of the station. As we listened to the message, in the background, it sounded like every crew member was laughing and having a great time.

Fearing something but not knowing what, my crew was evacuated Earthside. A contingent of U.S. Space Marines took our place. From Copernicus, using Jump Ships, they made their way to Icarus.

The squadron reported an odd discovery before they entered the base. It appeared that some type of viscous material covered everything, even the moon's surface, making it a gummy mess that clung to their pressure suits. This made movement and working with equipment difficult. Once they did make their way inside, things became even more strange. The Marines reported that the Icarus crew were all there and seemed to be unharmed despite being covered with some sort of gel-like material.

They almost looked as if they were sleeping. All had smiles on their faces.

Shortly before we lost touch with the squadron, they laughed hysterically about the situation.

Instead of sending another squadron to investigate further, the U.S. Space Force ordered the Marines to destroy Moon Base Icarus. The soldiers were reluctant to do this with some of their mates inside. Still, no one wanted to go in and look for them, so the base was vaporized. Then the soldiers came home.

In a few days, we realized that something had followed closely behind them.

It started at the bottom of the world. There are no permanent residents in Antarctica, no indigenous population, nothing like that. However, anywhere from 7 to 10 nations, including the United States, maintain research bases on the continent. A week after the Space Marines successfully returned to Earth, America's Amundsen–Scott South Pole Station research station, located near the geographical South Pole, sent an alarming string of transmissions. The first one stated that the snow on the ground around the station and the snow falling from the sky had turned green.

The next one included a collection of pictures confirming that mint-colored snow covered the grounds around the station and that the snow falling from the sky matched its color.

The final transmission was a video, 5 minutes and 43 seconds in length, showing the scientists and staff outside in the stuff. They were all naked, and their skin bore a greenish tint. They were building snowmen and throwing snowballs. Some were even lying in the snow, making love.

As the video ended, a voice off-camera told us not to be afraid.

Eventually, every station on the continent that had not been evacuated sent transmissions that followed the same pattern.

Alarm, curiosity, giddiness, and a message telling us not to be afraid.

To them, all was well with the world.

Then silence.

Since I was the lone remaining Astrobiologist on the moon when the odd incidences transpired in Moon Base Icarus, I was dispatched to Antarctica to investigate. Thanks to the Navy having ships at the ready, I survived the expedition, though we lost most of our party.

As soon as we flew over Antarctica proper, our CMV-22B, which had lifted off the deck of an aircraft carrier sitting 200 miles off its coast, began to have trouble. The pilots could not understand why. All systems were reading normal, but the plane started losing altitude despite having fully functioning engines. It was as if the propellors could not create any displacement in the thick green air above the snowy landmass. Instead, they slid through it like a knife cutting jelly.

After turning back, just before we skidded into the Southern Ocean, I thought the tint in the air outside of the plane's cabin reminded me of mint jelly.

When the crew of a Navy Cutter stationed halfway between the continent and the aircraft carrier pulled me from the icy water, I was suffering from severe hypothermia. Hence, I have no memory of how my transport to Washington, D.C., was accomplished. I awoke a week later in the ICU unit of Walter Reed National Military Medical Center.

I was 20 miles from the White House and only a few miles from my home on the outskirts of Somerset, MD.

No sooner had I opened my eyes when the Deputy Secretary of Homeland Security came to see me. I was surprised. I worked for his boss but had not voted for the man.

He was very agitated and appeared to be deeply worried. After he filled me in on what happened on Earth while I was insensible, I understood why.

Nearly one-third of the population on the planet had gone silent.

Everything, every person, every animal below the 30th Parallel was dead. No communication was possible. High-resolution satellite images of South Africa showed people lying in streets, parks, job sites, and every other place where humans gathered.

All of the faces that could be seen were adorned with a smile. All the bodies were covered with a mint green film.

Many were holding each other, regardless of who they appeared to be. All seemed very happy to be doing so. The images, which the Secretary showed me on his tablet, were very peaceful. There were no signs of violence in any of them.

Everything seemed right with the world, even though everyone in the pictures was probably dead.

No one above the 30th Parallel knew that for sure.

The Secretary then told me that hundreds of scientists of varying degrees and I were being moved to a high-security location somewhere around North Lake, North Dakota. The plan was to assemble a massive think tank equipped with all the latest technology to find out what was happening on Earth and then find a way to stop it. The President personally ordered me to go because I was respected in my field of study. I was also the only person who had been to both the moon and Antarctica when these strange events began. That was fine with me. I wanted to study the phenomenon anyway.

Just not in a crowd.

Still, I decided to not tell the Secretary that I wasn't going with the rest. He'd find out soon enough.

Feigning sickness, which was not hard to do, I told him that I would not be well enough to leave for a few days. He wanted to argue, but my doctor put an end to that. He said a move like the one the President proposed might kill me. I wasn't sure if it would or not, but I figured that if I could not find a way to stop what was happening, I would be dead anyway.

I would stay one more night in Walter Reed. Then I would go home and work in my bunker laboratory, where I could think clearly without all the noise and arguments that would be the only product of the government's think tank.

I had a theory about what caused the green snow that I was not quite ready to share in circumstances like that.

I never married. No one wanted a workaholic companion whose life's goal was to go to the moon. Nor did they want one so consumed with their profession that they spent a substantial amount of money creating a state-of-the-art lab in their basement, complete with a small clean room and an airlock for the door.

I kept my lab well stocked with food and drink, too. Extra clothing, two Moon suitable pressure suits with spare air tanks, and a few hundred N95 Particle Respirator masks filled a small closet. I had a cot for a bed. I could live there and work there for months, and if I died down there, no one would know or care.

So, I stalled for time, but I knew I couldn't wait too long. I had to get on with it.

The next night, while the ICU was quiet, I dressed and snuck out of Walter Reed.

They came to my house looking for me, but they didn't find my carefully concealed lab door after breaking in. I had not taken anything from inside the house to the bunker, so it still had an air of disuse. A thin layer of dust covered most of the furniture.

After a few days, they gave up. There were more pressing matters that needed their attention.

I wouldn't know if my theory was correct until I had a sample of the material I'd seen in the air over Antarctica. I felt confident that it was also the substance the Marines found on everything when they inspected Moon Base Icarus. I was also sure that the material was in some way related to the ORCs, if for no other reason than their color. Because I was now a fugitive of sorts, I knew that the government would not give me a sample, so I would have to wait until it reached D.C.

Since it spread over a third of the planet in a week, I knew it would not be a long wait.

Two days after leaving the hospital, reports on the waning internet declared that all communication with any country below the Equator had been lost. By the next day, Mexico had blanked out. This showed me, in Earth time, just how badly we underestimated ORCian speed. Not that it would matter much if there were no way to stop them from engulfing our world.

By the next day, or the one after that at the latest, they would swallow D.C.

I needed to get ready.

Standing inside my front door, dressed in my pressure suit with my pack ready, I noticed a light green buildup around its edges. Most likely, my house would be filled with ORC before long, but the functioning airlock to my lab should keep it at bay while I looked for a way to stop its spread.

In the past few hours, as I readied my equipment, I thought that maybe I should just let it go. Perhaps this is the way that mankind should end. Peaceful and happy just before death. It would be far better than dying in a nuclear war or needing a ventilator to keep breathing as the latest version of COVID-19 ravaged your body. Perhaps I was playing God in my mind, I don't know. What would a real God do? Maybe He is the one behind all of this anyway.

Whatever the case, I opened my door, quickly stepped outside, and slammed it closed behind me.

Walking was difficult. My boots could get no purchase on slimy green sidewalks. Staying on grassy surfaces was better, but not by much. It was a good thing I didn't need to go too far to find what I needed.

Because of my government position, I had long ago been given access to the internal Homeland Security database. While the information now being entered into it about the ORCs was spotty, I learned that no signs of contagion were associated with it. I didn't expect any, but I was happy to hear this. It allowed me to use a simple sterile plastic Petri dish to gather some of the green material instead of bulkier specimen gathering equipment. It also freed me from using my air tanks since the heavy-duty N95s would keep the slime from touching my skin.

I had a syringe to draw blood.

When I arrived at a nearby park, I looked for a healthy young man. Preferably one with well-developed arms where I could easily find a vein. I knew that many athletes used the park to run and work out, so I easily found such a person.

The man I stood over was older than I wanted, but he appeared to be a bodybuilder. His veins bulged pleasingly just below his massive biceps. Before drawing blood, I used a small plastic spoon to scrape some of the invading substance off his well-developed pectoral muscles, then I transferred it to a Petri dish.

Stashing the specimen in my pack, I took out the syringe. It was not easy to handle in my pressure suit, but I didn't have to be too precise. The man wouldn't feel a thing.

Without thinking about it, I pulled his arm closer to where I knelt. I missed the man's vein on the first and second try, but on the third try, I collected a few drops, which is all that I would need.

It was then that the horror of the situation struck me!

I had easily moved his arm! There was no sign of rigor mortis, not the slightest, and yet there should be--if he were dead. More, the three punctures I made in his arm began to ooze blood which meant that his heart was beating.

The man was alive!

As I staggered back from the body, I looked around at the other people in the park. A young mother with a baby in her arms, two old men slumped over a spilled chessboard, a pair of lovers lying peacefully on a blanket, ducks floating in the pond.

They must all be alive, too!

But how? Why? What had put them in this state?

Rattled, I gathered my specimens and headed home as quickly as the slippery footing allowed.

Before I went to my lab, I set my pack in my bathroom sink, turned on the shower until steaming hot water poured out of it, then stepped in to wash off all the green residue that clung to my pressure suit, the syringe, and the Petri dishes. When I was sure it had all gone down the drain, I toweled everything dry and then went to my basement lab.

The blood analysis result was startling, but it clarified one thing. It explained why this was all happening but not how it was happening. That answer came from the analysis of the ORCian fluid. Now I knew everything. It was all clear to me. I needed to sit down, think it through, then decide on my next move.

So I put on my pressure suit, turned off the lights in my lab, and walked back to the park.

I went past the man's body I'd violated with my needle. The blood on his arm had coagulated, stemming its flow. He would die, but not due to anything I did. Looking around at my fellow humans, I knew they too would eventually die, but none of them would know it. I felt some comfort in knowing that they would never be subjected to dying a slow death from disease. Knowing that they won't have to perish in agony due to some calamity. Knowing that old age would not kill them as it stole their humanity one piece at a time.

No, they would all die just as they are now. Smiling and happy.

I found an unused bench by the pond, watched the ducks floating, head up, with their bills tucked under their wings. I sat for a long time trying to decide if I would die with them.

The blood I'd drawn disclosed a near toxic, but not fatal, level of alcohol in it. The man and I have to assume the rest of those in his state were rendered unconscious by it. Based on his blood-alcohol level, I determined that no human body could ingest enough distilled spirits to reach the level that I found in the man's blood. It could have only reached that level if it had been absorbed through the skin. It was almost like he had been floating in a vat of pure alcohol.

Then there was the matter of the type of alcohol I'd found.

It took a few days of researching and running tests to determine that it was Perilyll alcohol, a naturally occurring monocyclic terpene most often found in plants, mainly green plants.

This could only mean that the pervasive, wet, green matter engulfing Earth was plant-based, and all of Earth's creatures were being saturated with the alcohol to the point of being eternally comatose.

When I opened the petri dish with the ORC specimen in it, the inside of the lid was tacky to my touch. It felt like drying glue, but, in fact, it was drying sap.

While sitting in my bed at Walter Reed, I theorized that ORCs were living creatures, moving randomly through space. I was correct to some extent, but they were not biological organisms such as men and animals. ORCs were autotrophic organisms that made their own food through photosynthesis.

They sustained themselves on sunshine.

Now, I determined that ORCs must be large drops of a sap-like substance searching for food while looking for the brightest spots in the universe. Our Sun must be one of their favorite places to visit, which is why they returned to it.

During my research, I also learned that traces of Perilyll alcohol were found in samples of petrified wood, some of which were over 225 million years old. The wood grew and likely absorbed some ORCian substance in the Late Triassic Epoch when many dinosaurs evolved. I conjectured that ORC sap was less toxic to dinosaurs than to Earthlings, or perhaps their reptilian metabolism fought off the effects of the ORC fluid. Maybe it was a combination of both that let them survive for millions of years before they eventually lay down and went to sleep.

It's also possible that ORCs have been to Earth several times in past eons.

I will never know.

Someday, if humans walk once more on this planet, they may find the answer.

For now, though, we were the new dinosaurs.

Sitting in my neighbor's van, I felt a pang of guilt about borrowing it even though he would never know I did. It was larger than my SUV, so it held more equipment than my small sports SUV.

I managed to get it into my garage and close the door before too much of the slime followed me inside. Still, I used a hose roughly attached to my kitchen sink to wash off what little residue made it onto the surface. I didn't want it touching me while I loaded my equipment into it.

I had a long drive ahead of me.

It could be that I was on a fool's errand, but giving up was not in my nature, so I backed out of my garage, said goodbye to my house, and turned in the direction of North Dakota. From what I could glean from the Homeland Security database, I had a good idea of where the think tank is located. If anyone is still conscious when I get there, they may have some answers.

If not, I would strip naked and run around until I dropped peacefully, knowing that the ORCs had not come to destroy us. We biological beings were just another casualty in nature's never-ending effort to survive.

In the end, the ORCs had come bearing only peace.

Die With Dignity
Tyree Campbell

The young woman blinked rapidly after the hood was removed. Nearer objects slowly came into focus—a floor lamp with a bright light aimed directly at her head; an empty cushioned chair with arms and casters; a wooden table on top of which stood some electronic equipment.

Finally the other objects in the room became clear. Faces meant people, a dozen of them at least, standing in a group. No one spoke; they just stood there, breathing. Beyond them a solid wall of indeterminate color. Faint light outlined the door in the wall, indicating the way in. And the way out.

She tried to move, but was only able to turn her head from side to side. Sitting; confined to a wooden chair by ropes of rough fiber; forearms secured to the chair arms, lower legs to the chair legs.

She was naked. Lank brown hair afforded her only a measure of non-strategic cover. For a moment she debated whether to jerk her head from side to side to cascade her hair to achieve for her a bit of modesty—it was long enough for that—but decided against it. Such a maneuver would only confirm to her captors that she felt uncomfortably vulnerable.

Danton—no weakness, she thought wryly, recalling the last words of a hero of the French Revolution, before his decapitation by the guillotine.

From the gathering came a harsh female voice. "What's your real name?"

Name, rank, service number, date of birth. She had only the first and last to give them. At the moment, she was willing to respond to her interlocutors. Accordingly, she answered, "Harper MacLeod."

"Liar!" someone called.

"Bitch," from another.

This from a third: "Lineage-ist!"

In the shadows beyond the pole lamp, a flat hand moved down as if to quiet the group. Harper did not respond. She had no way to confirm her identity, and had simply answered truthfully. She had nothing to conceal from them . . . yet.

"I'll ask you only one more time," called the female voice. "Your true name?"

"Harper MacLeod."

From the group flew a tomato. It splatted against her left kneecap. It seemed a waste of vegetable, with folks starving here in northern Calivada, but she withheld this observation.

"Name-shamer!"

"Hater!"

Again the disembodied hand and arm gestured, quelling the outburst. The limb grew into a young man who emerged from the shadows. Who chose to stand just to one side of the lamp, where she would be unable to make out any of his features in detail. Rule by namelessness, she thought, recalling the slogans of equality. Rule by democracy. Silently she added two of her own to the litany. Rule by mob. Rule.

Her shoulders rose and fell just a little with her weary sigh. Soon enough it would all be over. There, if she could get there; here, if she had to provoke them.

"Afraid of light, sonny?" she asked him, her disparagement calculated to measure the hostility of the group. Was physical violence their ultimate design, or did they mean to compel her social adjustment in exchange for her release?

"Age-ist!"

"Youth-shamer!"

The young man stepped further aside, so that she could see his features: unruly dark hair and hard eyes; a delicate nose that would have been easy to break, had she been unconfined and had she the will; pale skin—he hadn't seen a lot of sunlight; a rail-thin body that was almost certainly the result of continuous food confiscations. She rather imagined the owners of the disembodied voices shared much the same physiques. Even in the wake of starvation, they remained true believers. Almost certainly she was looking at members of the Congress of Students that ran the nearby People's Pacific Union College

He took two steps forward, bringing him halfway to her. "Can you see me now, Harper?" he sneered.

"That would be Ms MacLeod to you."

In response she heard gasps of speechlessness. A head of squishy lettuce struck her on the shoulder.

Finally someone found her voice. "Genderist!"

And another: "Gender shamer."

For long seconds the young man remained silent, as if he were permitting the little throng behind him to vent before he took charge once again.

Even in ubiquitous and enforced equality, Harper reflected, there is always someone in charge.

The young man took a folded sheet of paper from a pocket of his dark jeans, and unfolded it to display before her, the very act itself an accusation. "This was found on you."

The printing on it reminded her of an eye chart. Larger letters in the first line, smaller in subsequent lines. The top line read: DIE WITH DIGNITY.

* * *

The logo on the pickup showed a woods beside a lake, with the reflection of the trees in the water. Surrounding the logo were the words CALIVADA FORESTRY. The pickup was parked at the perimeter of an open field northeast of Calistoga. Here, near the border between Napa and Lake Counties, had thrived some of the grape vines that had fed the wine industry since the 1800s. By the direction of Calivada's Prima Inter Pares, affectionately known as PIP, the land had been fallowed at first, following a massive dose of still-uninvestigated arson, and then planted in Douglas fir, beech, black walnut, oak, and butternut—the last three intended to service a horde of squirrels that had staked a claim in the area. The field itself, however, consisted of sparse grassland over somewhat rocky terrain, the lack of understory possibly due to the field's proximity to the Old Faithful Geyser of Calivada. Geologically the land was active.

Forestry Ranger Gordon 5 had been asked by the Congress of Students that ran the nearby People's Pacific Union College to look into the rumors of deaths in the field.

Forestry Ranger Gordon 5 was the offspring of Vintner Linda 283, and in most other lands of the DSA he might have been known as Gordon Lindason, Gordon Howe (following his paternal lineage) or even Gordon Ranger, as occupations had often served as family names in the deep past. Not, however, in this area of northern Calivada. A trend had begun around the time of his birth and was still a work-in-progress. It had developed after the realization that to acknowledge one's ancestors was lineage-ism, and in some cases tantamount to racism.

In all of Calivada, he was the only Forestry Ranger Gordon 5. There being no other way to distinguish him by identity, and in the interests of diversity, no occupation, including that of ranger, was allowed within its ranks more than one individual of any particular name.

Forestry Ranger Gordon 5 exited his pickup and began a casual exploration of the general area. Grassland was grassland, and he detected nothing noteworthy about the field. Some of the blades reached as high as his hips, and the clumps were dense enough that he had to force his way over them. Here and there, burrs stuck to the fabric of his green uniform trousers. Off to his left, a bird, startled by his presence, took wing, its protests fading in the distance. Off to his right . . .

About fifty meters off to his right walked a girl who looked old enough to be in high school. She was wearing an aqua tank top that made her long and loose yellow hair stand out. The height of the grass made it difficult to determine her lower garment, but a few flashes of tan skin told Forestry Ranger Gordon 5 it might be blue jean cutoffs.

She strode as if she knew exactly where she was going, and why. Ahead of her was a little rise, after which the terrain gave way to a down slope and denser grass before leveling off as it reached the surrounding treeline. She leaned forward into the climb, and came to a halt at the top of the rise. Her gaze drifted past Forestry Ranger Gordon 5 without settling on him; he was no more than an object she had taken note of before moving on.

Forestry Ranger Gordon 5 started to raise his arm and call out to her, and held back. It was not illegal for her to be there, nor was she in any particular danger. He had not been given a uniform and a shield in order to indulge in whimsy.

The girl moved down the slope. From his angle of view, he could see the upper half of her body. About halfway down, she stopped again. Once more she looked around, her eyes passing over him without interest. She took one more step forward, and disappeared. A sheet of paper fluttered from her hand and sailed into the grass.

* * *

"Where did you get this?" demanded the young man, thrusting the paper at Harper.

"In the diner," she answered. "On the table where I ate my ham and eggs."

Horrified gasps from the audience followed.

"Islamophobe!"

"Carnivore!"

Harper smiled. "A pleasant young man about your age handed it to me," she added.

"Heterophile!"

"Homophobe!"

The young man before her waved his hand, and the tumult waned. Again he showed her the flier, and pointed to the second line. "What's this?" he asked.

She shrugged. "Thirty-eight fifty double-zero, one twenty-two forty double zero."

"I can read!"

"So why are you asking me to read for you?"

He slapped her cheek. It stung briefly. Several in the audience cheered, and encouraged more.

A pale girl with tangled mousy-brown hair stepped forward and spat on Harper. "Hater!" she yelled, before retreating.

"And this?" said the young man, pointing to the third and last line. It read: "Just jump right in."

Harper shrugged again. "That's what I was hoping to find out."

* * *

In a corner office of a great cube of cut brown stone and concrete block in the center of Nova Santa Rosa in northern Calivada, an austere young woman made several circuits around her gray steel desk, a relic of the previous century, muttering as she walked. A robot sitting in a folding metal chair beside the desk recorded her every distinguishable word. Whenever the woman raised her voice the robot twiddled her own nipple nodes, aware that the woman found such erotic movements calming and even alluring. The robot, an object of metal and silicon and silicates and a dash of rare-earth metals, had not been designed for attraction, but for record-keeping competence. It was the woman who'd had programmed into her a rudimentary personality.

"*No comprendo, no comprendo, yo no comprendo,*" said the woman, pausing behind her desk to pick up her Palmetto. The robot's left hand returned to her nodes.

The woman was known as PIP, or Prima Inter Pares, and her task was to administer to northern Calivada under the auspices of the federal government in Sacto. The name that appeared on her employment records was Fries-maiden Amparo, the same name under which she had been appointed by Sacto to administer the northwestern quadrant of the country. She was given ironhand authority to do this. The great cube structure had housed several PIPs before her, but she was the only one who had a ForLife clause in her appointment. Sacto itself had little interest in a land populated primarily by protected trees.

What PIP did not understand was numbers. Specifically, declining numbers. She checked the figures on her Palmetto for the fifth time, as if expecting them to change. Every individual in Calivada had been chipped from birth and accounted-for. Chips expired at death, their numbers factored into the totals. Everyone entering the country was chipped at the border. The chip even noted when an individual departed from Calivada, and took that into account at the end of each month when conducting the census. Sacto used the figures to determine the proper amount of money to dole out to each of its provinces.

Northwest Calivada was losing population. It would receive less federal money from Sacto.

Fries-maiden Amparo chucked the Palmetto back onto the desk. Disgust tarnished the olive-brown skin of her face as she stared hard at the robot. The reduction in population was hardly the robot's fault, but that mattered not at all to PIP. "Robotic Associate Roberta, how can we have a reduction of population when no one has left the country?" she demanded, in thickly-accented English.

"*I would like a slinky for my birthday.*"

Someone knocked at the office door. Amparo marched up to it and slid it open. "What?"

A male in janitorial gray—coveralls, shirt, and boots, all of natural plant fiber—looked taken aback by her abruptness. "I clean you office," he sputtered, in broken English. The name tag sewn onto his shirt read Janitorial Associate Javier 119.

PIP sighed. There was always something. The Juana Azurduy Office Complex comprised six levels, each with thirty-six offices. A janitorial staff of forty people—eighteen males and twenty-two females—serviced the 216 offices. 215, amended PIP; she'd had a wall knocked out in order to combine two offices, so that she might have additional window space and, thereby, sunlight. Of the 214 remaining offices, some seventeen were in use, including one where the janitorial staff changed clothes, another that served as a utility closet, and a third as a break room, complete with vending machines that provided purified water and various kinds of granola bars.

She sighed again. You'd think that with 215 offices and six levels, the staff could find somewhere else to clean.

"Come back later," she snapped, and started to close the door.

"You no unnerstand," Janitorial Associate Javier 119 protested. "No clean, no pay. My family they live on sidewalk. No home. No job, not eat."

"Everyone has a job here," she recited. "And a place to live. I'll be done here at four. Come back after that."

The janitor shook his head. "I wash car then. Two job."

PIP glared at him. "You *wash* them?"

"No use water," he said quickly. "Use duster. I dust them."

"That's better. All right, come in here. Make it quick."

* * *

Forestry Ranger Gordon 5 ran toward the spot where he had last seen the girl. The uneven terrain and clumps of grass and even an occasional barrel cactus impeded his progress, and over two minutes had transpired by the time he reached the site. There was no sign of the girl. She had literally disappeared from the face of the Earth.

The sheet of paper she had carried now was caught in the foliage of a dry shrub. Forestry Ranger Gordon 5 pulled it free and read it. The three lines made absolutely no sense to him. Still, he had witnessed . . . something; he was not sure what. He had no choice but to call it in.

* * *

Register Clerk Tyler 359 glowered at the ordering screen in the lobby of the *Arcos de Oro* fast-food restaurant. His mumbled comment elicited a question, which he explained to his three companions at the table.

"It's dehumanizing. People need confidence that their orders will be filled as desired, not as specified. You order a meal with coffee. You want one cream and one sugar. The machine orders the meal with coffee, but you have to have face time with an attendant in order to have the cream and sugar added."

"That's a tempary glitch, *no mas*," said Swedish Masseuse Pedro 7. "Silicon Valle make new sof'ware, ¿*verdad*?. You get cream sugar."

Register Clerk Tyler 359 looked dubious. "I've been using that same order machine for," he paused to calculate, "sixteen years now. It hasn't changed."

"Money, homs," said Electricity Meter Reader Supervisor Elrod 16. Chewing a bite of Grilled Chicken Wrap from a Healthy Meal with Treat tended to abbreviate his speech. "You going to buy a cuppa *somewhere*. It's all same-same. No choice. Ergo, no new software."

"Not the point," muttered Register Clerk Tyler 359. He sat back, exasperated. "Look, population growth is outpacing job growth. Tech advancements displace workers. It's like spending past the card limit. At some point, the system must collapse. Either we stop replacing people with machines, or we stop and then reduce population growth. Someone tell me just how we can stop people from fucking."

"Luddite," sneered Russian-English/English-Russian Interpreter Hideki 2, half in jest. "Where did you go to grad school, anyway?"

"People's Sympath College of Los Angeles," replied Register Clerk Tyler 359. "What does that matter? I'm still right."

"You went to PisCola?" said Swedish Masseuse Pedro 7, and shook his head. "*Pobrecito*."

"How come you work in a store, homs?" asked Electricity Meter Reader Supervisor Elrod 16.

"There's not a lot of jobs in astrophysics, is how come."

A disturbance at the restaurant entrance changed the subject. All four males turned to look. Meal Assembly Technician Marcela 28 was remonstrating with what by appearances was an older male who called sidewalks home. They caught snippets of dialogue that suggested the male had come begging for food and Meal Assembly Technician Marcela 28 was disinclined to grant the request.

"I wasn't aware of a housing shortage," was the comment from Russian-English/English-Russian Interpreter Hideki 2. "Why would anyone choose to live on the street when they could have a nice, warm, cozy apartment?" He fished out the last of the pineapple chunks from a fruit tray. "Makes no sense."

"You'd think he would at least choose to die with dignity," said Electricity Meter Reader Supervisor Elrod 16.

At this, Register Clerk Tyler 359 was aghast. "Why'd you say that?" He tried to scoot his chair back, but it was bolted to the floor. "What made you say that? That's not a solution! Not a solution at all!"

"Easy, hombre," soothed Swedish Masseuse Pedro 7. "He don' mean nothing by it. Don' be scared."

"I'm not scared! I just...I just don't like that, that phrase. What made him say that? What made you say that? I'm not scared. Not scared at all."

* * *

Former Fries-maiden Amparo, now known as PIP, stepped out the front door of the Juana Azurduy Office Complex and headed for the *Tofu Paradise* just down the avenue. The night air was chill, and only a few dimmed street lights dotted the darkness. She reached the corner of the Complex, and came to a stop at the crosswalk, where she pushed the button on a pole to signal the lights network that a pedestrian wished to cross the street. Two E-cars whined past while she waited for the correct light to appear. A red light stopped cross-traffic. Turn-signal lights allowed vehicles to turn, but there were none in queue at the intersection. Full lights came, allowing all other traffic to proceed, of which there was none. Meanwhile, PIP shifted her weight from one leg to the other and back, anxious to continue on to the natural foods restaurant she favored. There was absolutely no traffic.

The full traffic lights eventually changed to yellow and then to red, at which point the bicycle lane lights turned green, allowing bicycle traffic to proceed, again of which there was none. PIP stomped her feet and muttered under her breath. She looked both ways: there was *nothing* on the streets. Finally [!] the bicycle lights turned red, and the pedestrian crosswalk lights turned green. She fairly ran across the street. Finally!

She walked swiftly past the corner Stop-n-cash kiosk, where one could receive an advance on a paycheck; past a former liquor store that now sold bottles of fresh, or purified, or flavored water; past what was once the Cottoner's and was now the Natural Fiber Clothing Store; and across an alley, where a hissed voice stopped her in her tracks.

"Yo, mama, wanna buy a straw?"

She turned to him, her voice hoarse with shock and horror. *"What did you say?"*

The man was wearing a dark hoodie and a gray baseball cap pulled down almost over his eyes. He tugged a plastic straw from a box and displayed it. "Hey, mama, it's a straw," he hawked. "You drink through it, right? Only ten *chavezes*, man. One crisp *tubman*. Good for water of any kind, y'know?"

"You," sputtered former Fries-maiden now Prima Inter Pares Amparo. "You *monster!*" She tugged a police whistle from under her blouse and put it to her mouth, blowing hard. "Police!" she screamed. "He's got straws. He has a straw." Again she blew, and again. *"Help, police!"*

The hoodied man gaped at her as if he were unable to believe that she was serious. Then he scampered down the alley and into the darkness. He did not see the two uniformed police officers come running.

Former Fries-maiden Amparo pointed with a shaky finger at the alley. "Down there," she fairly shrieked. "Be careful. He has *straws*. Don't let him get away."

The two officers drew weapons and flashlights and headed into the alley. Satisfied that she had done her civic duty, Fries-maiden Amparo continued on her way. Moments later, she heard gunfire, and took a moment's satisfaction in knowing that she had helped to save the environment.

* * *

"Where did you get this?" snarled the young man.

Harper MacLeod mulled over several possible responses, and settled for the truth. That, she hoped, might force the hand of this young, rabid mob. They would have to kill her, or let her go. Either way, the end result would be the same.

"It was on a stack on a counter at a bookstore."

Gasps of horror shot throughout the room. When the onlookers recovered, they issued fresh epithets.

"Murderer!"

"Tree-killer!"

"Truth-hater!"

MacLeod laughed. "Truth-hater?"

"There are no bookstores," snapped the young man. "They're illegal! You're lying! Where is it?"

"If I am lying," she replied, her calm a counterpoint to his agitation, "if there are no bookstores, then it is nowhere."

"*Where?*"

She shrugged. It made no difference now. "In the basement of a private home in Sacto," she told him. "It moves daily. It might be in Davis today, frex, or in Placerville. Maybe in Napa."

That seemed to puzzle the young man. "Why would it be moved at all?"

"For security reasons." She was tempted to add, "Duh!" but it would have given her only a momentary pleasure and have elicited a painful or vegetable response.

She was wondering whether he would ask the obvious question, when he did so, surprising her. "Wait. How do you know where this bookstore will be each day?"

"She lies!" someone shouted. "All books are digital."

The young man waved this off. He now reminded MacLeod of a ferret having caught the scent of prey. Probably he thought to receive a reward for this vital information he was about to obtain.

"There is an underground organization," she said quietly. She could almost imagine the little *frissons* of fear scurrying up the spines of the students from the People's Pacific Union College. "It has no name, nor does it need one," she went on.

"We read Plato, J. D. Salinger, James Baldwin, Ayn Rand, Robert Heinlein, James Madison, Maya Angelou, Franz Kafka, Alice Walker, Voltaire, H. G. Wells—"

"Old white men!"

"Racists!"

"Counter-revolutionaries!"

"White privilege!"

The young man turned to confront the onlookers. He raised his hands as if to push them away. "I will handle this," he said firmly. "This is now a matter of state."

"Every once in a while one of us turns up an old book and puts it into the store to be rented," MacLeod went on, ignoring the interruption. "We call it a bookstore, but it's more like a library. As to how we know where to go, we use short-wave radio."

The young man's eyebrows bunched. "Short-wave radio? What is that?"

MacLeod smiled without mirth. "Exactly."

The chant from the onlookers then began: "Two four six eight we don't read white men who hate!"

* * *

Register Clerk Tyler 359 remained volatile and frightened. His shaking hand tipped over a recycled-paper cup of water, sloshing himself with the contents. "Why would anyone want to die?" he asked, the question obviously rhetorical, for none of his companions responded. "It isn't like that at all. Sure, there are always questions and glitches, like with the cream for the coffee, but this is the best world, the best possible...how could you give it up? It doesn't make sense!"

Electricity Meter Reader Supervisor Elrod 16 cleared his throat. "Take it easy, Register—"

Register Clerk Tyler 359's voice became more strident. "This is what we wanted! This is what my ancestors wanted —"

"Keep your voice down," hushed Swedish Masseuse Pedro 7. Palms down, he made a plea for calm. "And don't be lineage-ist."

"It's what they wanted! Now we have it! We *all* have it. We have done it. We have created the most splendid society in all the history of humankind!"

The expression on the face of Russian-English/English-Russian Interpreter Hideki 2 sobered, his lips taut in disapproval. "Register Cler—"

"My name is Tyler Robinson!" roared Register Clerk Tyler 359. "I am not a number. I am not a job. I am...am..." Suddenly the air went out of him. "Oh, fuck," he moaned, and clapped his hands to his head as he sank back into his chair.

* * *

The work day over, an exhausted and grime-smeared Janitorial Associate Javier 119 returned in the dark to the clump of pest-ridden blankets that had become part of the sleeping quarters and breakfast nook for himself and his family. The claim he had staked to this part of the sidewalk was being encroached by a rough-looking man with a black beard as ridden as the blankets. Maternal Careprovider Soledad 13173 looked to Janitorial Associate Javier 119 with fear in her haunted, dark eyes as she clutched the two children to her, as protectively as she was able.

Janitorial Associate Javier 119 now had no choice. He dipped into a pocket of his ragged and grimy coveralls and came up with a *tubman*. This represented half his day's earnings. He passed it to the bearded man, who folded it and tucked it away.

"See you tomorrow," he said, and slipped away into the dark.

* * *

"...six eight we don't read..."
"I would like my clothes back now," said Harper MacLeod.
"Body-shamer!"
"I have answered—"
"...who hate. Two four six..."
"...stions as best I could. I assure—"
"Lies. White promises!"
"...read white men..."
"...mean no harm to anyone. I just want—"
"I, I, I." a female voice cried out. "It's always about you. Never about us."
"...to be on my way."

The young man raised his hand, and swept it to one side. The chanting faded and stopped.

"Return her clothing," he ordered. "And release her."

* * *

"I don't know where she went, Forestry Ranger Supervisor." Having raised headquarters in Nova Santa Rosa, Forestry Ranger Gordon 5 was speaking into the radio in his jeep. "She was there one second, and gone the next. All I found was a sheet of...well, of paper, Forestry Ranger Supervisor."

"That's evidence of a crime, Forestry Ranger Gordon 5. You'd better turn it over to Forensics. We'll have to find out where it came from."

"Yes, Forestry Ranger Supervisor. Of course." He hesitated.

"Was there something else?"

"Ah...yes. It says Die With Dignity."

A despondent sigh soughed through the jeep. "Not another one..."

* * *

It was, thought MacLeod, a veritable clandestine parade. A hundred yards (not meters) off to her right, her interlocutor stood with a skinny, mousy young woman, trying to look like they were out for a nature hike, and casting furtive glances her way. A uniformed man, possibly a ranger, sat on the fender of a jeep some fifty yards to her left, openly observing. And beside her...

Moments ago she had turned at the sound of dried grass crunching to find a wiry man dressed in work brown drawing up to her. He was not in the surveillance parade. In his left hand he carried a folded sheet of blue paper. When he saw that she had spotted him, he stopped, and smiled ingratiatingly.

"Tyler Robinson," he said, and stuck out his hand.

She took it. "Harper MacLeod."

He gave her a look of mock surprise. "What? No occupation? No number?"

She laughed. "And you."

They resumed walking, in silence at first, until Robinson cleared his throat. MacLeod went on edge: she was not sure she wanted to discuss what she was about to do.

"What was it for you?" he asked.

The question was direct yet innocuous. Her tone held a shrug. "I refused to live under these conditions, in this society," she said. "But there was nowhere else to go. The United States was the last chance. When it fell to those... people, that was the end of it." She stepped over a dead branch, and helped him over it. "They won't understand that, of course. They cannot conceive of such rejection. But death is better than this. And it will be my way, and my choice." She paused, and turned around. "You?"

He was studying his Palmetto. "GPS," he explained. "We're almost there."

She held up her own device, and grinned. "I know."

He put his away. "What do you think we'll find?"

"Escape," she said. "Freedom."

"For me, it was my identity. I am me, not a device of their own creation."

"Bravo."

"Seriously."

She laughed, the light sound of a bird warbling. "I am serious." Suddenly she held out her arm, barring his progress. "Whoa!"

They had reached a point between two hummocks where the rough grass gave way to nothing at all. The hole reminded MacLeod of the entrance to an abandoned mine shaft, except that this one seemed to go straight down. She peered into it.

Beside her, Robinson said, "I can't see the bottom."

"There may not be one."

"But-but I don't speak Chinese."

She laughed, this time a guffaw. "I doubt we'll pass through the Earth." She looked around. None of the watchers had made any move to interfere with her and Robinson; they seemed to know that something was about to happen, but had no idea what it might be.

"Just jump right in, it says," read Robinson, and refolded the paper. "What do you suppose is down there?"

"Release," she answered. "Poe's surcease of sorrow. Death. There has to be a bottom down there somewhere."

"Maybe...it's like, you know, a portal."

"Maybe so. Does it matter?"

"Not in the slightest."

They glanced at one another. Neither had to ask whether the other was ready. Smiling now, she took his hand.

www.ingramcontent.com/pod-product-compliance
Lightning Source LLC
LaVergne TN
LVHW012034060526
838201LV00061B/4603